The Watcher & Other Stories

Also by Italo Calvino

Cosmicomics

t zero

Italo Calvino

THE
WATCHER
&
Other
Stories

A Helen and Kurt Wolff Book
Harcourt Brace Jovanovich, Inc., New York

AUTHOR'S NOTE: *The substance of* The Watcher *is based on fact, but the
characters are all entirely imaginary.*

Contents

1   The Watcher
(1963)

75   Smog
(1958)

139   The Argentine Ant
(1952)

The
Watcher

Translated by William Weaver

AMERIGO ORMEA left his house at five thirty in the morning. It looked like rain. To reach the polls where he was to act as an election watcher, Amerigo followed a series of narrow, arcaded streets, still paved with old cobblestones, along the walls of humble buildings, densely inhabited, no doubt, but still without any sign of life on that Sunday at dawn. Unfamiliar with the neighborhood, Amerigo deciphered the street names on the sooty signs—names perhaps of forgotten benefactors—tilting his umbrella to one side and raising his face into the rain dripping from the eaves.

The members of the opposition (Amerigo Ormea belonged to a left-wing party) generally considered rain on election day a good omen. This notion dated from the first postwar election, when people still believed that in bad weather many Christian Democrat voters—people with no great interest in politics, old people, disabled, infirm, or living in country areas with poor roads—wouldn't stick their noses out of their front doors. But Amerigo didn't share this illusion: it was 1953 now, and in all the elections in subsequent years he had seen that, rain or shine, the organization to get out the vote always worked. And today of all days, when the parties in the coalition government had to put over a new election law ("the swindle law," as the other parties had christened it), whereby if the coalition got 50-plus-1 per cent of the votes it would receive two-thirds of the seats in Parliament . . . For his part, Amerigo had learned that change, in politics, comes through long and complex processes, and you couldn't hope for change overnight, as if it were a stroke of luck; for him, as for so many others, acquiring experience had meant becoming slightly pessimistic.

On the other hand, there was the moral question: you had to go on doing as much as you could, day by day. In politics, as in every other sphere of life, there are two important principles for a man of any sense: don't cherish too many illusions, and never stop believing that every little bit helps. Amerigo didn't seek the limelight; in his profession, he preferred to remain the right man in the right place, not pushing himself forward. And in public life, as in his work, he wasn't what you could call a "politician," either in the good sense or the pejorative. (Because the word "politician" did have a good meaning or a pejorative one, depending on how you looked at it: Amerigo was well aware of this.) He was a paid-up member of the party, true enough, and though he could hardly be considered an "activist," as his nature tended toward a quiet life, he never hung back when there was something useful to be done that lay within his capacities. At the local cell, they considered him a sound man, with a good background; and now they had appointed him a poll watcher, a modest assignment, but a serious, necessary job, especially at this particular polling place, which was set up inside a great religious institution. Amerigo had accepted willingly. Now it was raining. His shoes would stay wet all day.

II

GENERIC TERMS like "left-wing party" and "religious institution" are not used here to avoid calling things by their real name but because even declaring, *d'emblée,* that Amerigo Ormea's party was the Communist party and the polls were located inside Turin's famous "Cottolengo Hospital for Incurables" would represent a more apparent than real progress toward precision. Each of us, according to his own knowledge and experience, attributes to the word "Communism" or the word "Cottolengo" various and even contradictory values, so even more precision would be required: the role of the party in that situation would have to be defined, in the Italy of those years, and Amerigo's position within the party; and as for "Cottolengo," otherwise known as the "Little Home of Divine Providence"—assuming that everyone knows the function of that enormous hospital, to shelter unfortunates, the afflicted, the mentally deficient, the deformed, even creatures who are hidden, whom no one can see—then it would be necessary to define Cottolengo's place in the citizens' pious sentiments, the respect it inspired even in those furthest from any religious feeling, and at the same time the quite different place it had come to occupy in pre-electoral polemics, almost as a synonym of fraud, of embezzlement, of prevarication.

In fact, ever since the vote had become obligatory in the period following the Second World War, hospitals, asylums, and convents had served as great reservoirs of votes for the Christian Democrat party, and at Cottolengo, above all, at each election instances were discovered of idiots being led to vote, or dying old women, or men paralyzed with arteriosclerosis, in any case, people unable to make logical distinctions. As a result of these instances, there was a crop of anecdotes, ranging from the burlesque to the pathetic: the voter who ate his ballot, the one who, finding himself in a booth with that piece of paper in his hand, thought he was in a latrine and behaved accordingly, or the line of slightly brighter retarded voters who entered the polls chanting the name of the candidate and his number on the ballot: "One two three: Quadrello! One two three: Quadrello!"

Amerigo knew all these stories and he felt no curiosity or amazement at them; he knew that a sad, nervous day was ahead of him; as he wandered in the rain, looking for the entrance number marked on the little card from City Hall, he felt he was stepping over the frontier of his world.

The institution sprawled among poor, crowded neighborhoods, covering as much space as a whole quarter of the city, including a complex of asylums and hospitals and homes for the aged, schools, convents, virtually a city within the city, surrounded by walls and governed by different rules. Its outline was irregular, a body that had become gradually extended through new bequests and constructions and enterprises: from over the walls rose the roofs of buildings, spires, treetops, and smokestacks. Where the public street separated one part of the institution from another, they were joined by overhead passages, as in certain ancient factories, which had sprung up according to the dictates of practical utility and not of beauty; these were the same, bounded by bare walls and gates. The factory idea went beyond the external resemblance: the same practical talents, the same spirit of private enterprise of the founders of the big industries had also inspired—though expressing the succor of outcasts rather than production and profit—the simple priest who between 1832 and 1842 had founded and organized and operated, despite difficulties and hostility, this monument to charity on the scale of the nascent industrial revolution; and even his name—Cottolengo, that simple rustic family name—had lost all individual connotation and had come to denote a world-famous institution.

. . . In the cruel speech of the poor, that name had become, by a natural process, a mocking epithet, meaning cretin, idiot, even abbreviated, in the Turin way, to its first syllables: *cutu.* In other words, that name "Cottolengo" united an image of misfortune with an image of comedy, of the ridiculous (as often happens, in popular speech, to the names of madhouses and prisons), and also an image of kindly providence, of the power of organization, and now, too, through its electoral function, an image of obscurantism, of the medieval, of bad faith. . . .

Each meaning faded into the next, and on the walls the rain was soaking the election posters, suddenly aged, as if their aggressiveness had died with the last evening of the political battle among meetings and billposters, the night before last, and as if these posters were already reduced to a patina of paste and cheap paper, where, layer upon layer, the symbols of the opposing parties could be read, transparently. At times the world's complexity seemed to Amerigo a superimposition of clearly distinct strata, like the leaves of an artichoke; at other times, it seemed a clump of meanings, a gluey dough.

Even in his calling himself a "Communist" (and in this journey he was making for the party, in the dawn as damp as a sponge) you couldn't tell how much was duty handed down from generation to generation (between the walls of those ecclesiastical buildings, Amerigo saw himself—half ironically and half seriously—as a final, anonymous heir of eighteenth-century rationalism, though with only a remnant of that heritage which had never borne much fruit in the city where Pietro Giannone was kept in irons) and how much was the outcome of another chapter of history, barely a century old, but already bristling with obstacles and restrictions: the advance of the socialist proletariat (then it was through the "inner contradictions of the bourgeoisie" or the "self-awareness of the declining class" that the class struggle had managed to bestir even the ex-bourgeois Amerigo), or the more recent incarnation of that class struggle, only about forty years old, as Communism had become an international power and the revolution meant discipline, preparation for responsibility, bargaining among powers even where the party wasn't in power (then Amerigo was attracted by this game many of whose rules seemed established and inscrutable and obscure, though you often felt you were helping establish them), or else, within this participation in the Communist movement, there was a faint reservation about general questions that led Amerigo to choose the more limited and modest party assignments as if recognizing that they were the most surely useful, and even in them he was always prepared for the worst, while trying to remain serene in his (another generic term) pessimism (also partly hereditary, that sigh-filled family air that marks the Italians of the non-Catholic minority, which, every time it wins, realizes it has lost), but always subordinate to a coexistent, stronger optimism, that optimism without which he wouldn't have been a Communist (then we should have said: a hereditary optimism, in the Italian minority which thinks it has won each time it loses; in short, the optimism and the pessimism were, if not the same thing, then opposite sides of the same artichoke leaf), and, simultaneously, subordinate to its opposite, the old Italian skepticism, a gift for adapting to circumstances and waiting (in other words, that minority's age-old enemy: and then everything became mixed up again because a man who sets out to make war on skepticism cannot be skeptical about his victory, cannot resign himself to losing, otherwise he is identified with the enemy), and above all, having finally understood what wasn't really so hard to understand: that this is only one corner of the immense world and that decisions are made— we won't say elsewhere, because "elsewhere" is everywhere —but on a vaster scale (and even here there were reasons for pessimism and reasons for optimism, but the former came more spontaneously to mind).

III

TO TRANSFORM a room into a polling place (a room that is usually a schoolroom or a courtroom, a refectory, a gymnasium, or a municipal office) only a few objects are required—those sheets of unpainted planed wood, which form the booth; that wooden box, also unpainted, which is the ballot box; the materials (register, packs of ballots, pencils, ballpoint pens, a stick of sealing wax, string, strips of gummed paper) which are given to the chairman at the moment that the "polls are legally opened"—and a special arrangement of the tables found on the spot. Bare rooms, in other words, anonymous, with whitewashed walls; and objects even more bare and anonymous; and those citizens, there at the table—chairman, clerk, watchers, perhaps some "district representatives"—also assume the impersonal appearance of their function.

When the voters begin to arrive, the scene becomes animated: the variousness of life enters with them, each one individualized by gestures too awkward or too brisk, voices too loud or too meek. But there is a moment, beforehand, when the election officials are alone, sitting there counting the pencils, a moment that rends the heart.

Especially where Amerigo was: the room assigned to this poll—one of the many established inside Cottolengo, because each district comprises about five hundred voters, and in all of Cottolengo there are thousands—was on normal days a parlor where relatives visited the inmates, and there were wooden benches all around the walls (Amerigo drove from his mind the facile images the place prompted: peasant parents waiting with baskets of fruit, sad conversations) and the tall windows overlooked a courtyard, irregular in shape, among pavilions and arcades, a bit like a barracks, a bit like a hospital (some women, who seemed too large, pushed carts, moved huge cans; they wore black skirts like the peasant women of long ago, black wool shawls, black bonnets, blue aprons; they moved swiftly in the fine rain that was still falling; Amerigo gave them a brief glance, then came away from the windows).

He didn't want to succumb to the room's squalor, and to avoid that he concentrated on the squalor of their electoral equipment—that stationery, those files, the little official book of regulations which the chairman consulted at the slightest doubt, and he was already nervous before they began—because, for Amerigo, this squalor was rich, rich in signs, in meanings, perhaps even contradictions.

Democracy presented itself to the citizens in this humble, gray, unadorned dress; to Amerigo there were moments when this seemed sublime; in Italy, which had always bowed and scraped before every form of pomp, display, sumptuousness, ornament, this seemed to him finally the lesson of an honest, austere morality, and a perpetual, silent revenge on the Fascists, on those who had thought they could feel contempt for democracy precisely because of its external squalor, its humble accounting; now they had fallen into the dust with all their gold fringe and their ribbons, while democracy, with its stark ceremony of pieces of paper folded over like telegrams, of pencils given to callused or shaky hands, went ahead.

There, around him, were the other officials, commonplace people, most of them (it seemed to him) mustered on the recommendation of Catholic Action but some (besides himself) from the Communist and Socialist parties (he still hadn't distinguished them), performing a common task, a rational, secular service. There they were, dealing with little practical problems: how to draw up the report on "Voters registered at other districts"; how to go over the tally for the district, taking into account the list of "Deceased Voters" that had arrived at the last moment. There they were, now using matches to melt some wax to seal the ballot box, and then they didn't know how to snip off the extra length of string, so they decided to burn it with a match. . . .

In these actions, in this identifying themselves with their temporary duties, Amerigo promptly recognized the true meaning of democracy, and he thought of the paradox of their being there together, some believers in a divine order, in an authority which is not of this earth, and then his own companions, well aware of the bourgeois deceit of the whole business; in short, two kinds of people who should have had little faith in the rules of democracy, and yet each side convinced they were its most zealous guardians, its very incarnation.

Two of the watchers were women: one, wearing a little orange sweater, seemed a factory worker or a clerk, about thirty, with a red, freckled face; the other was fiftyish, with a white blouse, a large locket with a portrait hanging over her bosom, perhaps a widow, an elementary school-teacher, to judge by her appearance. Who would think, Amerigo said to himself, now determined to see everything in the best possible light, that women have enjoyed their civil rights for so few years? They looked as if, daughter following mother, they had never done anything but prepare for elections. And what's more, it's the women who show the most common sense, good at little practical problems, helping the men, who are more self-conscious.

Following this train of thought, Amerigo was already content, as if it were all going for the best (apart from the dark prospects of the elections, apart from the fact that the ballot boxes were in an asylum, where they had been unable to hold political meetings, or stick up posters, or sell newspapers), as if this were already the victory, in the old struggle between State and Church, as if this were the triumph of a lay religion of civic duty, over . . .

Over what? Amerigo looked around once again, as if seeking the tangible presence of a contrary force, an antithesis, but he could grasp nothing, he could no longer set the affairs of the polls against the atmosphere that surrounded them: in the quarter of an hour he had been there, things and places had become homogeneous, joined in a sole, anonymous, administrative grayness, the same in police stations and regional offices as in the great charitable institutions. And like a man who, diving into cold water, has forced himself to believe that the pleasure of diving is in that sensation of cold, and then, swimming, has found within himself a new warmth and, with it, the sense of how cold and hostile the water really is, so Amerigo, after all his mental efforts to transform the polls' squalor into a precious value, had gone back to his first impression—of an alien, cold place—and he felt that this was the correct view.

In those years, Amerigo's generation (or rather, that part of his generation that had lived in a certain way during the years after '40) had discovered the resources of a previously unknown attitude: nostalgia. And so, in his memory, he began to contrast the scene before his eyes with the atmosphere of Italy after the liberation, in those few years whose most vivid recollection now was the way everyone had taken part in political affairs and actions, in the problems of that moment, serious and elemental (these were thoughts of the present: then he had lived as if the atmosphere of those times was natural, as everyone did, enjoying it—after all that had happened—angry at things that were wrong, without ever thinking they could be set right); he remembered how people looked then, all of them seeming equally poor, and interested in universal questions more than in private ones; he remembered the makeshift party offices, filled with smoke, with the rattle of mimeograph machines, with people in their overcoats outdoing one another in volunteer work (and this was all true, but it was only now, when years had gone by, that he could begin to see it, to make an image of it, a myth); he thought that only that newly born democracy deserved the name "democracy"; that was the value which, a little while ago, he had been seeking vainly in the humility of objects and hadn't found; because that period was over now, and the field had slowly been occupied again by the gray shadow of the bureaucratic State, the same before, during, and after Fascism, the old gap between the managers and the managed.

The voting which was about to begin would (Amerigo was, unfortunately, sure) lengthen this shadow, widen this gap, it would drive those memories still further back, until they became less and less substantial and harsh, and more and more ethereal and idealized. So the Cottolengo visiting parlor was the perfect setting for the day: wasn't this room perhaps the result of a process similar to democracy's? In the beginning, here too (in a period when poverty was still without hope) there must have been warmth in the piety that filled people and things (perhaps there was even now— Amerigo didn't want to deny that—in individual persons and places in the institution, separated from the world), and between the outcasts and their benefactors there must have been created the image of a different society, where life, and not self-interest, was what mattered. (Like many nonbelievers, looking at things from the historical view, Amerigo made a point of understanding and appreciating developments and forms of religious life.) But now this was a huge institution, a complex of hospitals, with certainly outdated equipment, which somehow performed its function, its services, and, what's more, had become productive, in a way no one could have imagined at the time of its foundation: it produced votes.

So is what matters, in everything, only the beginning, the moment when all energy is tensed, when only the future exists? Doesn't the moment come, for any organization, when normal administrative routine takes over? (For Communism, too—Amerigo couldn't help wondering—would it happen with Communism, too? Or was it already happening?) Or . . . or are institutions, which grow old, of no matter; is what matters only the human will, the human needs which go on being renewed, restoring verity to the instruments they use? Here, to establish the polls (now they had only to tack up in a prominent position—according to the regulations—three notices: one with the laws concerned, and two with the lists of candidates), those men and

14

women, strangers and in part hostile to one another, were working together, and a nun, perhaps a Mother Superior, was helping them (they asked her if they could have a hammer and a few tacks), and some women inmates, with checked aprons, peeped in curiously, and "I'll get them!" a girl with a huge head cried, pushing past the others. She ran off laughing, came back with hammer and tacks, then helped them move a bench.

Her excited movements revealed, in the rainy courtyards beyond, a whole participation, an excitement at this election, as if for an unexpected feast day. What was it? What was this care in tacking up properly those notices, like white sheets (white, as official notices always seem, even with all their black print which nobody reads), which united a group of citizens, all surely "a part of the productive life," with these nuns, and the poor girls who knew nothing of the outside world except what could be seen from an occasional funeral procession? Amerigo now felt a false note in this common effort: in them, in the election officials, it resembled the effort you make during military service to carry out the assigned tasks whose ends remain alien to you; in the nuns and inmates it was as if they were preparing trenches all around, against an enemy, an attacker: and this election bustle was the trench, the defense, but in some way also the enemy.

So when the officials were at their table, waiting, in the empty room, and when the little group outside of people who wanted to get their voting over with quickly began to move, and when the municipal guard began to let the first ones in, all of them felt the certainty of what they were doing, but also a hint of absurdity. The first voters were some little old men—inmates, or artisans employed by the institution, or both at once—a few nuns, a priest, some old women

(Amerigo was already thinking that these polls might not be too different from others): as if the opposition brooding behind it all had chosen to present itself in its most reassuring aspect (reassuring for the others, who expected the election to confirm the old positions; depressingly normal, for Amerigo), but no one felt reassured by it (not even the others), and all sat there instead waiting for some presence to make itself known from those invisible recesses, perhaps a challenge.

There was a lull in the flow of voters, and a footstep was heard, a kind of hobbling, or rather a banging of planks, and all the election officials looked toward the door. In the doorway a little woman appeared, very tiny, seated on a stool; or rather, not exactly seated, because she didn't touch the floor with her feet, nor did her legs sway, nor were they folded under her. They weren't there, her legs. This stool, low, square, a footstool, was covered by her skirt, and below —below her waist, and also below the woman—it seemed there was nothing: only the legs of the stool could be seen, two vertical sticks, like the legs of a bird. "Come in!" the chairman said, and the little woman began to advance, that is she thrust forward one shoulder and a hip, and the stool shifted obliquely on that side, and then she thrust out the other shoulder and the other hip, and the stool made another quarter-turn to catch up; and fixed to her stool in this way, she dragged herself across the long room to the table, holding out her voter's certificate.

IV

YOU BECOME accustomed to anything, and more quickly than you think. Even to watching the inmates of Cottolengo vote. After a while, it seemed the most usual, monotonous sight to those on this side of the table; but on the other side, among the voters, the emotion of the exceptional event, the breaking of the norm, continued to spread. The election itself had nothing to do with it: who understood that? The thought that filled them was apparently the unusual public appearance required of them, inhabitants of a hidden world, unrehearsed to play the protagonist's part before the inflexible gaze of outsiders, representatives of an unknown order. Some of the voters suffered, morally and bodily (stretchers carried in some patients, while others, lame or paralyzed, hobbled forward on crutches), some displayed a kind of pride, as if their existence had finally been recognized. In this pretense of freedom that had been imposed on them, was there also, Amerigo wondered, a glimmer, a presage of real freedom? Or was it only the illusion, for just a moment and no more, of being there, of displaying oneself, of having a name?

It was a hidden Italy that filed through that room, the reverse of the Italy that flaunts itself in the sun, that walks the streets, that demands, produces, consumes; this was the secret of families and of villages, it was also (but not only) rural poverty with its debased blood, its incestuous couplings in the darkness of the stables, the desperate Piedmont which always clings to the efficient, severe Piedmont, it was also (but not only) the end of all races when their plasm sums up all the forgotten evils of unknown predecessors, the pox concealed like a guilty thing, drunkenness the only paradise (but not only that, not that alone), it was the mistake risked by the material of human race each time it reproduces itself, the risk (predictable, for that matter, on a calculable basis, like the outcome of games of chance) which is multiplied by the number of the new snares: the viruses, poisons, uranium radiation . . . the random element that governs human generation which is called human precisely because it occurs at random. . . .

And what, if not random action, had placed him, Amerigo Ormea, a responsible citizen, an aware voter, a participant in democratic power, on this side of the table, and not on the other side, like that idiot, for example, who came forward laughing, as if it were all a game?

When he was opposite the chairman, the idiot snapped to attention, made a soldierly salute, and held out his documents: identity card, electoral certificate, all in order.

"Good," the chairman said.

The other man took his ballot, the pencil, clicked his heels once more, saluted, and marched confidently toward the booth.

"These are fine voters, all right," Amerigo said aloud, though he realized the remark was banal and in bad taste.

"Poor things," said the woman in the white blouse, adding then: "Well, in a way, they're blessed. . . ."

Swiftly, Amerigo thought of the Sermon on the Mount, of the various interpretations of the expression "poor in spirit," and then of Sparta and Hitler, who did away with idiots and the deformed; he thought of the concept of equality, according to the Christian tradition and the principles of '89, then of democracy's century-long struggle to establish universal suffrage, and of the arguments that reactionary polemics opposed to it, the thought of the Church, first hostile, then favorable; and now of the new electoral mechanism of the "swindle law," which would give more force to this idiot's vote than to his own.

But wasn't this implicit evaluation of his own vote as superior to the idiot's also an admission that there was some logic in the old anti-egalitarian argument?

The "swindle law" was nothing. The trap had been sprung long since. The Church, after years of refusal, had taken at face value the equal civil rights of all citizens, but it replaced the concept of man as protagonist of History with that of Adam's flesh, wretched and ill, which God can nonetheless save through Grace. The idiot and the "responsible citizen" were equal before the omniscient and the eternal; History had been restored to the hands of God; the dream of the Enlightenment had been checkmated when it seemed to win. Election watcher Amerigo Ormea felt he was a hostage, captured by the enemy army.

V

THE WATCHERS spontaneously arrived at a division of labor: one sought out the names on the register, another crossed them off the voting list, a third checked the identity cards, one directed the voters to this or that booth, depending on which was free. A natural understanding among them was quickly formed, so they could carry out these tasks as rapidly as possible, without confusion, and there was even a kind of tacit alliance with regard to the chairman, elderly, slow, afraid of making mistakes, whom they had to urge on, all together, with determination, each time he was about to be swamped by details.

But beyond this practical division of tasks, another division was taking shape, the real one, which set them against one another. The first to give herself away was the woman in the orange sweater; she began nervously to make objections because of an old woman who came out of the booth, waving her ballot, unfolded. "Her vote's no good! She showed her ballot!"

The chairman said he hadn't seen anything. "Go back into the booth and fold your ballot now, right and proper," he said to the old woman, and to the watcher: "You have to be patient. . . ."

"The law is the law," the woman insisted harshly.

"But she meant no harm . . ." said another watcher, a thin, bespectacled man. "You could close an eye. . . ."

"We're here to keep our eyes open," Amerigo might have said, at that point, to support the woman in the orange sweater, but he felt a desire to close his own eyes, as if that procession of inmates gave off a hypnotic fluid, as if it made him prisoner of a different world.

For him, an outsider, it was a uniform procession, mostly of women, and he had a hard time distinguishing differences among them: there were those who wore checked aprons and those in black with bonnet and shawl, and the white nuns and the black nuns and the gray nuns, and those who lived at Cottolengo and those who seemed to have come there just to vote. Anyway, they were all alike to him, ageless old bigots, who voted in the same way, amen.

(Suddenly he imagined a world where beauty no longer existed. And it was female beauty he thought of.)

These girls with their hair in braids, orphans perhaps or foundlings brought up in the institution and destined to remain there all their lives: at thirty they still had a slightly infantile look, he couldn't tell whether it was because they were backward or because they had always lived there. You would have said they went straight from childhood to old age. They resembled one another like sisters, but in each group there was one who stood out, the brightest, the dutiful one, explaining endlessly to the others how the voting procedure worked, and when there were some who had no documents, she would sign for them, swearing to their identity, as the law allows.

(Resigned to spending the whole day among those drab, colorless creatures, Amerigo felt a yearning need for beauty, which became focused in the thought of his mistress Lia. And what he now remembered of Lia was her skin, her color, and above all one point of her body—where her back arched, distinct and taut, to be caressed with the hand, and then the gentle, swelling curve of the hips—a point where he now felt the world's beauty was concentrated, remote, lost.)

One of the "bright" girls had already signed for four others. Then came another of the women all in black, Amerigo couldn't tell if they were nuns or what. "Do you know anyone?" the chairman asked her. She shook her head, dismayed.

(What is this need of ours for beauty? Amerigo asked himself. Is it an acquired characteristic, a linguistic convention? And what, in itself, is physical beauty? A sign, a privilege, an irrational stroke of luck, like—among those girls— their ugliness, deformity, deficiency? Or is it a gradually shifting model we invent for ourselves, more historical than natural, a protection of our cultural values?)

The chairman urged the woman on: "Look around. See if somebody knows you and can identify you."

(Amerigo thought that instead of being there he could have spent Sunday in Lia's arms, and this regret didn't now seem to contradict his sense of civic duty which had led him to act as watcher: to make sure the world's beauty doesn't pass in vain, he thought, is also History, civic action. . . .)

The little woman in black looked around, all at sea, and then the same "bright" girl sprang forward and said: "I know her!"

(Greece . . . Amerigo was thinking. But isn't placing beauty too high in the scale of values also a step toward an inhuman civilization, which will then sentence the deformed to be thrown off a cliff?)

"Why, she knows them all, that girl does!" The shrill voice of the woman in orange rose. "Mr. Chairman, ask her if she can give you the voter's name."

(For thinking of his friend Lia, Amerigo now felt he should apologize to this beautyless world which for him had become reality, while Lia appeared in his memory as unreal, a shade. All the outside world had become a shade, a mist, while this one, inside, the Cottolengo world, so filled his experience that now it seemed the only real one.)

The "bright" girl had come up and was taking the pen to sign the register. "You know Battistina Carminati, don't you?" the chairman asked in one breath, and the girl promptly answered: "Oh yes, yes, Battistina Carminati," and she signed the register.

(A world, Cottolengo, Amerigo thought, that could have become the only world in the world if the evolution of the human species had reacted differently to some prehistoric cataclysm or some pestilence . . . Who could speak of the backward, deformed, idiots, today, in a world that was totally deformed?)

"Mr. Chairman! What kind of identification is that? You told her the name yourself!" The orange woman was enraged. "Try asking Carminati if she recognizes the other girl. . . ."

(. . . A path evolution might yet take, Amerigo reflected, if atomic radiations do act on the cells that control the traits of the species. And the world might become populated by generations of human beings who for us would be monsters, but who to themselves will be human beings in the only way that beings are human. . . .)

The chairman was already bewildered. "Well, do you know her? You know who she is?" he asked, and nobody could say to whom he was speaking now.

"I don't know, I don't know," the woman in black stammered, frightened.

"Of course, I know her; she was in the Sant' Antonio ward last year, wasn't she?" the "bright one" protested, twisting her face toward the watcher in the orange sweater, who replied: "Then ask her to tell us your name!"

(If the only world in the world were Cottolengo, Amerigo thought, without another world outside, which, in exercising its charity, overwhelmed and crushed and mutilated it, perhaps this Cottolengo world too could become a society, begin a history of its own. . . .)

The thin watcher also spoke out against the woman in the orange sweater. "They both live here; they see each other every day. They must know each other, mustn't they?"

(They would remember that humanity could be a different thing, as in fables, a world of giants, an Olympus. . . . As we do: and perhaps, without realizing it, we are deformed, backward, compared to a different, forgotten form of existence. . . .)

"If they don't know each other's name, then it isn't valid," the orange woman insisted.

(The more he was overcome by the possibility that Cottolengo might be the only possible world, the more Amerigo struggled not to be swallowed up by it. The world of beauty was fading on the horizon of possible realities like a mirage, and Amerigo went on swimming, swimming toward the mirage, to reach that unreal shore, and before him he saw Lia swimming, her back level with the surface of the sea.)

"Well, it seems I'm the only one here who is interested in respecting the law . . ." the orange woman said, looking around, vexed. In fact, the other watchers were examining their papers, as if they were concerned with something quite different, as if they were trying to discard the problem, opposing it only with an absent attitude, faintly annoyed, and Amerigo was doing the same, Amerigo who was there for the specific purpose of giving her a hand: he was at sea, among distant thoughts, as if in a dream. And in his waking part, he reflected that, in any case, the others would have their way and would allow voters without identification to cast their ballots anyhow.

Supported by the thin watcher, the chairman found the strength to emerge from his uncertainty and say: "I think the identification is valid."

"May I put my opposition on record?" the woman said, but the very fact that she asked it as a question was already an admission of defeat.

"There's nothing to put on record," the thin man said.

Amerigo moved behind the table, past the orange woman's back, and said softly: "Take it easy, comrade. We'll wait." The woman looked at him, questioningly. "It isn't worth making an issue of this. Our moment will come." The woman calmed down. "We must raise a general objection."

VI

FOR A moment Amerigo was pleased with himself, with his calm, his self-control. Perhaps this was what he wanted to be his behavior's constant norm, in politics as in everything else: mistrust of enthusiasm, synonym of naïveté, as of factional rancor, synonym of insecurity, weakness. This attitude of his corresponded to a habitual tactic of his party, which he had promptly assimilated, as psychological armor, to dominate alien, hostile situations.

However, as he thought about it, wasn't this desire of his to wait, not to intervene, to aim at a "general objection," dictated by a feeling of futility, of renunciation, by a basic laziness? Amerigo already felt too discouraged to hope he could assume any initiative. His legalitarian battle against irregularities, fraud, hadn't yet begun, and already that wretchedness had overwhelmed him like an avalanche. If they would only hurry it up, with all their litters and crutches, if they would only get it over with, this plebiscite of all the living and the dying and perhaps even the dead: with the limited formalities he could summon to his aid, no election watcher could stop the avalanche.

Why had he come to Cottolengo? Respect for legality? Ha! One had to start again from the beginning, from zero: it was the fundamental meaning of words and institutions that should be debated, to establish the most helpless person's right not to be used as an instrument, as an object. And this, today, in the present situation, when the elections at Cottolengo were mistaken for an expression of the will of the people, seemed so remote that it could be invoked only through a general apocalypse.

Extremism, like an air pocket, was, he felt, sucking him down. And, with extremism, he could excuse his sloth, his indifference, he could immediately salve his conscience: if he could remain silent and motionless in the face of an imposture like this, if he was almost paralyzed, it was because in such situations it was all or nothing, either you accepted them or else: *tabula rasa.*

And Amerigo shut himself up like a hedgehog, in an opposition that was closer to aristocratic hauteur than to the warm, elementary partisanship of the people. In fact, the nearness of other members of his party, instead of giving him strength, infected him with a kind of irritation, and when the woman in orange spoke up, for example, he was seized by a contrary reaction, as if he were afraid of resembling her. His thoughts raced in such an agile objectivity that he could see with the adversary's own eyes the very things he had felt contempt for a moment earlier, only to swing back, then, and feel with greater coldness how right his criticism was, and, finally, to attempt a serene judgment. Here again he was inspired not so much by a spirit of tolerance and of solidarity with his neighbor as a need to feel superior, capable of thinking all that was thinkable, even the adversary's thoughts, and capable of reaching a synthesis, of perceiving everywhere the patterns of History, according to the prerogative of the true, liberal spirit.

In those years the Italian Communist party, among its many other tasks, had also assumed the position of an ideal liberal party, which had never really existed. And so the bosom of each individual Communist could house two personalities at once: an intransigent revolutionary and an Olympian liberal. The more schematic international Communism became, in those hard times, the more explicit its official, collective expressions became, the more the militant individual lost inner richness, to conform to the compact, cast-iron block, and the more the liberal, housed in the same individual, gained new, iridescent facets.

Was this perhaps a sign that Amerigo's true nature—and the true nature of many like him—would have been, if left to itself, a liberal's, and that only a process, precisely, of identification with what was different, enabled him to be considered a Communist? Asking himself this question, for Amerigo, was like asking himself what was the essence of an individual identity (if such a thing ever existed . . .), beyond the external conditions that determined it. To weld in him—and in so many like him—those various metals was "the task of History," he thought—in other words, a fire beyond them (which went beyond individuals, with all their weaknesses). . . .

That fire glowed, however faintly, even in those polls, in all present there, and gradually it was revealed in each, varying in its degree of intensity, in the individual temperature they ran in playing their parts: Amerigo's vacillation, the orange woman's impatience (she was a member of the Socialist party, as he learned the moment they could go off to one side and talk), the thin, young Christian Democrat's need to believe that he was (even if there was no need) on a battle line, surrounded by enemies, the chairman's apprehensive rigidity, caused by his tenuous conviction in the system, and, for the woman in the white blouse (who overlooked no opportunity to underline her disagreement with the other woman), a need to feel edified and protected from the scandal of disobedience.

As for the others at the polls (all of them Christian Democrats, or further to the right), they seemed concerned only with smoothing over the differences: all of them knew that everyone in here would vote the same way, didn't they? Then why become upset, why look for trouble? There was nothing to do but accept things as they were, friends or enemies.

Among the voters, too, the importance of what they were doing varied. For the majority the act of voting occupied a minimal space in their awareness, it was a little "x" to make with the pencil against a printed symbol, something that had to be done, as they had been taught, with great care, like the proper way to behave in church or to make their beds. With no suspicion it could be done any other way, they concentrated their effort on the practical act, which was in itself—especially for the invalids or the mentally deficient—enough to engage their complete attention.

For others, more emotional, or indoctrinated in a different didactic system, the election seemed to take place in the midst of perils and deceit; everything was to be distrusted, a source of offense or fear. Certain nuns in white habits were especially obsessed with the idea of spotted ballots. One would go into the booth, stay in there for five minutes, then come out without having voted. "Have you voted? No? Why not?" The nun would then hold out the ballot, open and unmarked, and point to a little dot, faint or dark. "It's got a mark on it!" she would protest, in an angry voice, to the chairman. "I want a new one!"

The ballots were printed on ordinary paper, greenish, made from a grainy pulp, full of impurities, spattered with printer's ink from top to bottom. Soon the officials learned that whenever one of those white nuns came to vote the scene of the rejected ballot would be repeated. They couldn't be convinced that these were only defects in the paper, and that their ballots wouldn't be invalidated because of them. The more the chairman insisted, the more stubborn the little nuns became: one—an old, dark nun, who came from Sardinia—actually flew into a rage. They must surely have been given God knows what instructions about the question of the stains or spots: they were to watch out, at the polls there were Communists who spotted the nuns' ballots on purpose, to spoil their votes.

Terrified, that's what they were, these little white nuns. And in trying to make them see reason, the officials were of one mind: in fact, it was the chairman and the thin supervisor who became the most angry, since they weren't trusted and were treated as perfidious enemies. Like Amerigo, they wondered what could have been said to those poor women, to frighten them so, what horrors they had been threatened with, descriptions of the menacing Communist victory, which might be caused by a single wasted vote. The glow of a religious war filled the room for a moment, then was extinguished in nothingness; and the performance of their task resumed its normal course, drowsy, bureaucratic.

VII

THE JOB assigned him now, in the division of labor among the officials of the polls, was to check the identity papers. Swarms of nuns came to vote, hundreds at a time: first the white ones, then the black. As far as documents went, nearly all of them were in order; often the identity cards had been issued just a few days before, brand new. In the weeks before the election, the registry officers must have worked night and day to furnish documents for entire religious orders. And photographers, too: photograph after photograph, passport size, passed before Amerigo's eyes, all the pictures equally divided into black and white spaces, the oval of the face framed by white coifs and by the trapeze of the pectoral, all framed in the black triangle of the veil. And what it meant was this: either the nuns' photographer was a great artist, or else nuns are especially photogenic.

Not only because of the harmony of that celebrated pictorial motif, the nun's habit, but also because the faces came out as natural, serene, and with a good likeness. Amerigo realized that this checking the nuns' documents was becoming, for him, a kind of spiritual repose.

When he thought about it, it was strange: as a rule, in

those little square photographs, ninety times out of a hundred the sitter has widened eyes, bloated cheeks, a mindless smile. At least that was how he always looked, and now, checking these identity cards, in photographs where he found the face tense, forced in an unnatural expression, he recognized his own lack of ease before the glass eye that transforms you into an object, his lack of detachment in his attitude toward himself, his neuroses, the impatience that prefigures death in the photographs of the living.

But not for the nuns: they posed in front of the lens as if their faces no longer belonged to them; and so they came out perfectly. Not all of them, of course (Amerigo now read the nuns' photographs like a fortuneteller: he could distinguish those who were still bound by earthly ambition, those moved by envy, by unextinguished passions, those who were fighting themselves and their fate): you had to cross a kind of threshold, forgetting yourself, and then the photograph recorded this immediacy, this inner peace and blessedness. Is it a sign that blessedness exists? Amerigo wondered (these problems were not familiar to him, and he tended to associate them with Buddhism, with Tibet), and, if it does exist, should it be pursued? Should it be pursued, to the detriment of other things, of other values, in order to be like these nuns?

Or like the total idiots? They, too, in their freshly printed identity cards, were happy and photogenic. For them, too, offering an image of themselves was no problem: did this mean that the goal which a nun's life attains, after a toilsome path, is given to idiots by nature, by chance?

Instead, those who remain at a halfway house, the afflicted, the misfits, the retarded, the neurotic, those for whom life is difficulty and alarm, are terrible when photographed: with those taut necks, those rabbity smiles, especially the women, who still cherish a residual hope of look-ing pretty.

They brought in one nun on a stretcher. She was young. Strangely, she was a beautiful woman. Dressed as if she were dead, her face, flushed, seemed composed, as in the religious pictures hung in churches. Amerigo would have preferred not to be drawn to look at her. They left her in the booth on the stretcher, with a stool nearby, so that she, too, could make her "x." Amerigo, while she was in there, had her photograph before him, on the table. He looked at it and was frightened. Even in its features, this was the face of a drowned woman, at the bottom of a well, shouting with her eyes, as she was pulled down into the darkness. He realized that everything in her was refusal, writhing: even her lying there motionless and ill.

Is it good to be blessed? Or is this anguish better, this tension that stiffens faces at the photographer's flash and makes us dissatisfied with the way we are? Always ready to make extremes meet, Amerigo would have liked to go on clashing with things, fighting, and yet achieve at the same time, within himself, a calm above it all. . . . He didn't know what he would have liked: he understood only how far he was, he and everyone else, from living as it should be lived the life he was trying to live.

VIII

THE ABUSES to which an opposition party's watcher can usefully raise objections during the balloting at Cottolengo are limited. To become angry because they allow idiots to vote, for example, doesn't achieve any great result: when the documents are in order and the voter is able to go into the booth by himself, what can be said? You can only let it go, perhaps hoping he hasn't been taught well and will make a mistake (though this occurs rarely) and will increase the number of invalid ballots. (Now that the batch of nuns was finished with, it was the turn of a horde of young men, resembling one another like brothers, with their twisted faces, dressed in what must have been their best suits, as they are sometimes seen filing through the city on a Sunday when the weather is fine, and people point to them: "Look at the *cutu.*") Even the woman in the orange sweater was almost solicitous with them.

The cases where you have to be more alert are when a medical certificate authorizes a half-blind woman, or a paralytic, or someone without hands, to be accompanied into the booth by an authorized person (usually a nun or a priest) who can make the "x" for her or him. With this system, many poor wretches, incapable of discrimination, who would never be able to vote even if they had the use of their eyes or their hands, are promoted to the rank of bona fide voter.

In such cases there is almost always a certain margin for doubt and protest—for example, with a certificate of very weak eyesight: the watcher can immediately raise a protest. "Mr. Chairman, this man can see! He can go and vote by himself!" the woman in orange would exclaim. "I held the pencil toward him and he reached out and took it!"

This was a poor man with a deformed neck and a goiter. The priest accompanying him was large, heavy, blunt-faced, a beret pulled down to his ears; his manner was harsh and practical, not unlike a truck driver's; he had been bringing voters in and out for some while. He held out the palm of his hand, vertically, with the document plastered over it, and he struck it with the other hand: "Medical certificate. It's written here that he can't see."

"He can see better than I do! He took two ballots, and then he noticed there were two of them!"

"You think you know better than the oculist?"

The chairman, to stall for time, pretended amazement. "What's the trouble? What's the trouble?" Everything had to be explained to him again from the beginning.

"Let's see if he can go into the booth by himself," the woman said. The man was already on his way.

"Oh no!" the priest said. "What if he makes a mistake?"

"Ha! If he makes a mistake it's because he isn't capable of voting!" the woman in orange replied.

"Why are you taking it out on this poor unfortunate man? Shame on you!" the other woman official, the one in white, said to the first woman.

At this point Amerigo intervened. "We could surely make a test, to see if his sight . . ."

"Is this certificate valid, or isn't it?" the priest said.

The chairman examined the paper up and down and from side to side, as if it were a bank note. "Oh, yes, it's valid. . . ."

"It's valid, if it tells the truth," Amerigo protested.

"Is it true that you can't see?" the chairman asked the man with the goiter. The man with the deformed neck looked up. He didn't speak; he began to cry.

"I object! They're intimidating the voter!" the thin watcher said.

"Poor creature," the older woman in white said. "Not a spark of compassion!"

"Since the majority of the watchers agree . . ." the chairman said.

"I object!" the orange woman said.

"So do I," Amerigo said.

"What's all this fuss?" the priest said to the chairman, curtly, as if angry with him. "Are you preventing a voter from casting his vote? Mr. Chairman, have you nothing to say?"

The chairman decided the moment had come for him to lose his temper, to fly into a rage, the most violent rage that could be mustered by the mild, whining man he was. "Why, why, why," he said, "why, what is this? What's come over you all? Why do you want to stop this man? They all live here, poor things, at the Little Home of Divine Providence, which took them in when they were mere babies! And now, when they want to show their gratitude, you want to prevent them! Gratitude to those who have given them nothing but kindness! Have you no feelings?"

"Nobody wants to prevent an expression of gratitude, Mr. Chairman," Amerigo said. "But we're here to administer a political election. We have to make sure that each voter is free to cast his ballot according to his own ideas. What does this have to do with gratitude?"

"What ideas do you expect them to have, except gratitude? Poor outcast creatures! Here they have people who are fond of them, who take care of them, and teach them! They want to vote. More than all those others outside! Because they know what charity really means!"

Mentally Amerigo reconstructed their idea, noted the implicit calumny ("They're trying to say that Cottolengo is possible only thanks to religion and the Church, and that the Communists would simply destroy it, and therefore the vote of these poor unfortunates is a defense of Christian charity . . ."), he was offended by it, and at the same time, confuting it, with a certain sense of superiority ("they don't know that ours is the only total humanism . . ."), he erased the insult as if it had never existed, all in the space of a second (". . . and that we and only we can organize institutions a hundred times more efficient than this one!"), but what he really said was: "I'm sorry, Mr. Chairman, but this is a political election, they must choose among candidates of various parties . . ." ("Don't start making political speeches at the polls!" the thin man interrupted him), ". . . they're not voting for or against the Cottolengo Institute. . . . And so, what you've been saying, the expression of gratitude . . . gratitude to whom?"

Until then, the priest had stood there listening, his chin on his chest, his heavy hands pressed to the table, looking up from beneath his beret; now he raised his voice:

"Gratitude to the Lord our God, that's what!"

Nobody said another word. They all moved in silence: the man with the goiter made the sign of the cross, the older woman in white nodded her head in assent, the orange one raised her eyes as if prepared to put up even with this, the clerk started writing again, and the chairman went back to checking the list, and so each of the officials returned to his task. Agreeing with the majority, the chairman allowed the priest to accompany the afflicted man into the booth; Amerigo and the Socialist comrade had their protest put on record. Then Amerigo went outside for a smoke.

IX

THE RAIN had stopped. Even from those desolate courtyards a smell of earth rose, of spring. A few climbing plants were in flower against a wall. Under one of the arcades a group of schoolchildren was playing, a nun in their midst.

A long sound was heard, perhaps a cry, beyond the walls, beyond the roofs: were these the cries, the groans, that people said rose day and night from the wards of the hidden creatures in Cottolengo? The sound was not repeated. Through the door of a chapel a chorus of women was heard. All around there was a bustle among the various polls set up in almost all the pavilions, in ground-floor or second-floor rooms. White signs with black numbers and arrows stood out against the columns, under the old blackened plaques with the names of the saints. Municipal guards went by, carrying briefcases filled with papers. The regular policemen dawdled, their eyes dull, seeing nothing. Watchers from other polls had come out, like Amerigo, to smoke a cigarette and stare up at the sky.

"Gratitude to God." Gratitude for their misfortunes? Amerigo tried to calm his nerves by reflecting (theology was not his forte) on Voltaire, Leopardi (his arguments against the goodness of nature and of providence), and then—naturally—on Kierkegaard, Kafka (the acknowledgment of a god beyond man's ken, a terrible god). The election, here, if you paid it some attention, became a kind of religious rite. For the mass of voters, but also for him: the supervisor's concern with possible frauds was finally trapped in a metaphysical fraud. Seen from here, from the depth of this condition, politics, progress, history were perhaps not even conceivable (we are in India), any human effort to modify what is given, any attempt to elude the fate that falls to a man at birth, was absurd. (This is India, it's India, Amerigo thought, satisfied at having found the key, but also suspecting that he was brooding over banalities.)

This assemblage of afflicted people could only be summoned, in politics, to testify against the ambition of human forces. This is what the priest meant: here any form of ac-

36

tion (including voting in the election) was modeled on prayer, every task carried out here (the work of that little shop, the teaching in that classroom, the treatment in that hospital) had only one meaning, a variation on the one possible attitude: prayer, that is, becoming part of God, or (Amerigo was venturing definitions) the acceptance of human smallness, adding one's own nothingness to the sum in which all losses are canceled out, assenting to a final, unknown end which alone could justify these misfortunes.

To be sure, once you admit that when you say "man" you mean a Cottolengo man and not man endowed with all his faculties (to Amerigo now, despite himself, came mental images of those statuary, forceful, Prometheus-like figures from certain old party cards), the most practical attitude became the religious attitude, establishing a relation between one's own affliction and a universal harmony and completeness (did this mean recognizing God in a man nailed to a cross?). So were progress, liberty, justice then only ideas of the healthy (or of those who could, in other circumstances, be healthy), ideas of a privileged class, not universal ideas?

Already the boundary line between the Cottolengo men and the healthy was vague: what do we have beyond what they have? Limbs a bit better turned, a somewhat better proportion in our appearance, a somewhat greater capacity for co-ordinating sensations and thoughts . . . not much, compared to the many things that neither we nor they manage to do or know . . . not much, compared to our presumption that we can construct our history. . . .

In the Cottolengo world (in our world which could become, or already be, Cottolengo), Amerigo could no longer trace the line of his moral choices (morality impels one to act; but what if the action is futile?) or his aesthetic choices (all images of man are antiquated, he thought, walking among those little plaster Madonnas, those saints; it was no accident that the painters of Amerigo's age had all turned to abstraction by now). Forced for one day in his life to consider the extent of what is called natural misfortune ("And I should be grateful that they've only allowed me to see the brighter ones . . ."), he felt the vanity of everything yawning at his feet. Was this what they called a "religious crisis"?

There you are, you step out for a moment to smoke a cigarette, he thought, and you're overcome with a religious crisis.

But something in him resisted. Or rather, not in him, in his way of thinking, but around him, in the very things and people of Cottolengo. Girls with pigtails bustled by with baskets of sheets (toward, Amerigo thought, some secret ward of paralytics or monsters); idiots filed past, in lines, commanded by one who seemed only a shade less of an idiot than the others (these so-called "families," he asked himself, with sudden sociological interest—how are they organized?); one corner of the courtyard was cluttered with plaster and sand and scaffoldings because they were adding another floor to one of the pavilions (how are the bequests managed? What percentage went into expenses, additions, and how much into increase of capital?). Cottolengo was, at once, the proof and the denial of the futility of action.

Amerigo's historical attitude was regaining strength; all is history: Cottolengo, these nuns going to change the sheets. (A history, perhaps, that has remained stationary at one point in its course, clotted, turned in on itself.) Even this world of the retarded could become different, and would certainly become so, in a different society. (Amerigo had only vague images in his mind: luminous institutions, ultramodern, model educational systems, memories of pictures seen in the newspapers, an atmosphere that was almost too clean, rather Swiss. . . .)

The vanity of everything and the importance of each action of each person were contained within the walls of the same courtyard. Amerigo had only to walk around it and he would encounter the same questions and the same answers a hundred times. So he might just as well go back to the polls; he had finished his cigarette; what was he waiting for? "A man who behaves well in history," he tried to conclude, "even if the world is Cottolengo, is right." And he added hastily: "Naturally, to be right is not enough."

X

A LARGE, black automobile came into the courtyard. The chauffeur, with his visored cap, hastened to open the rear door. An erect, clean-shaven, gray-haired man stepped out. He was wearing a light raincoat, the kind with many buttons and loops, and the collar half turned up. People sprang into action, the policeman saluted.

The thin watcher asked the chairman in a low voice, ahem, since the Member of Parliament who was his party's candidate had arrived could he step out for a moment because he wanted to go just for a moment you understand to report how things were proceeding here.

The chairman answered in a low voice, ahem, to wait because since Members of Parliament are entitled to enter all the polling places perhaps the Honorable Member would come in here too.

And he did come in. The Honorable Member moved through Cottolengo with self-confidence, haste, efficiency, and euphoria. He inquired about the turnout of voters, he uttered a few words of kindly greeting to the voters waiting in line, as if he were paying an official visit to a summer camp for slum children. The thin watcher went over to say something to him: probably that the Communists were making difficulties, and how was he to behave with them when they wanted to put everything on record all the time. The Member barely listened to him, because he wanted to know only what was absolutely indispensable about what went on in here, and he didn't want to dwell on details. He made a vague, circular gesture, as if to say the machine was turning anyway, and turning well, there were millions of votes, and in these rather prickly situations, if a thing's done promptly, well and good: otherwise, let it go, skip it and pass on!

Then, abruptly, he asked about someone, flinging his questions to left and right: "Where is the Reverend Mother? Where is she?" and he went out into the courtyard again. The Mother Superior, informed, was already on her way to him; he went toward her, spoke to her as an old friend and as if he were jokingly giving her a scolding.

He chose to continue his tour of the various polls with the Mother Superior accompanying him. A little retinue followed him, mostly local candidates of the various districts (every so often one of the men would step forward, to tell him of some difficulty) and boys acting as messengers for the party (rushing back and forth with lists of voters transferred to other institutions but still entitled to vote here, or in any case, people for whom transportation had to be arranged), and the Member would give brief orders, unleash the messengers, the chauffeurs, answering everyone, taking him by the arm or clasping his elbow, to encourage him but also to thrust him promptly away.

At a certain point the cars for transporting voters had all gone off to collect people. A few messengers were dawdling, waiting to make another trip; the Member didn't like to see people standing idle, so he sent them off with his own car. Thus, each of them having been given a job, his retinue had dwindled. The Member found himself alone in the courtyard, and he had to wait until his car came back. The sun filled half of the sky; but still, in spurts, a few raindrops fell from the clouds. The Member stood for some moments in the solitude that kings and the mighty feel when they have finished issuing orders and see the world revolving on its own. He cast a cold, hostile look around him.

Amerigo was watching him through a window. And he thought: "As far as that man's concerned, Cottolengo doesn't even graze the lapel of his raincoat." (Catholic pessimism about human nature could be recognized beneath the Member's open manner, but Amerigo preferred to see it as lucid cynicism.) And he thought, too: "He's a man who likes his food, who smokes with a cherrywood cigarette holder. Perhaps he has a dog and goes hunting. Surely he likes women. Maybe he went to bed last night with a woman who isn't his wife." (Perhaps it was only Catholic indulgence toward his own gray conscience, as a good bourgeois paterfamilias, that gave the man his youthful look, but Amerigo chose to see him as a pagan, epicurean spirit.) And all of a sudden his aversion was transformed into solidarity: weren't they perhaps, the two of them, more alike than any of the others in here? Didn't they belong to the same family, the same side, the side of earthly values, politics, practicality, power? Weren't they both desecrating the Cottolengo fetish, one using it as an electoral machine and the other trying to unmask it in this function?

Looking out of the window, he noticed, at another window sill, two eyes that appeared behind the pane, a head that could only reach up as far as the nose, a huge skull covered with down: a dwarf. The dwarf's eyes were staring at the Member, and stubby little fingers were raised against the window's glass, the wrinkled palm of a tiny hand, striking against the pane, striking twice, as if to call him. What did the dwarf have to tell the man? Amerigo wondered. What was he thinking, the dwarf, of that authoritative personage? What was he thinking, he asked himself, of us, of all of us?

The Honorable Member turned, his gaze went to the window, lingered only a moment on the dwarf, then moved off, far away. Amerigo thought: "He has realized there is one who can't vote." And he thought: "He doesn't even see him, he doesn't deign to glance at him." And he also thought: "There, the Member and I are on one side, and the dwarf on the other," and he felt reassured by this.

The dwarf rapped his little hand against the window once more, but this time the Member didn't even turn around. Surely the dwarf had nothing to say to the man, his eyes were only eyes, without thoughts behind them, and yet you would have thought he had some message to communicate, from his wordless world, his world without relationships. What judgment, Amerigo wondered, can a world deprived of judgment pass on us?

The sense of human history's vanity which had come over him a little earlier in the courtyard seized him again: the realm of the dwarf overcame the realm of the Member, and now Amerigo felt entirely on the dwarf's side, he identified with Cottolengo's testimony against the Parliamentarian, against the intruder, the only real enemy who had infiltrated this place.

But the dwarf's eyes rested, with the same absence, on everything that moved in the courtyard, Member included. Denying value to human powers implies the acceptance (or the choice) of the worse power: the realm of the dwarf, having demonstrated its superiority over the Member's realm, annexed it, made it its own. And now dwarf and Member confirmed that they were on the same side, and Amerigo could stay there no longer, he was excluded. . . .

The black automobile returned and unloaded its freight of trembling little old women. With great relief, the Member took refuge inside the car, rolled down the window to issue some final incitements, and then left.

XI

AT NOON the flow of voters began to thin out. At the polls they agreed on taking turns in leaving, so some of the watchers who lived nearby could slip home for a bite to eat. Amerigo's turn came first.

He lived alone, in a little apartment; a woman came in by the hour to clean up and do a bit of cooking. "The Signorina telephoned twice," the woman said. He answered: "I'm in a hurry; give me something to eat right away." But there were two things he wanted more than food: to take a shower and to sit for a moment with a book open before his eyes. He took the shower, dressed; in fact, he changed his suit and put on a clean shirt. Then he drew his armchair over to the bookcase and started looking through the lower shelves.

His library was limited. As time went by, he had realized it was best to concentrate on a few books. His youth had been full of random, insatiable reading. Now maturity led him to reflect, to avoid the superfluous. With women it had been the opposite: maturity made him impatient; he had had a succession of brief, absurd affairs, all of them, as he could tell from the beginning, mistakes. He was one of those bachelors who, from habit, like to make love in the afternoon and, at night, to sleep alone.

The thought of Lia, which, all morning, as long as she remained an unattainable memory, had been necessary to him, was now irksome. He should telephone her, but talking to her at that moment would undo the web of thoughts he was slowly weaving. In any case, Lia would soon call him again, and before hearing her voice, Amerigo wanted to begin reading something that would channel and accompany his reflections, so that he could resume their train after the phone call.

But he couldn't find a book that met his needs, among the ones he had there: classics, haphazardly assembled, and modern writers, especially philosophers, a few poets, some books of cultural interest. Lately he had been trying to avoid pure literature, as if ashamed of his youthful vanity, his ambition to be a writer. He had been quick to understand the error concealed in it: the claim to individual survival, having done nothing to deserve it beyond preserving an image, true or false, of oneself. Personal literature now seemed to him a row of tombstones in a cemetery: the literature of the living as well as of the dead. Now he sought something else from books: the wisdom of the ages or simply something that helped to understand something. But as he was accustomed to reason in images he went on picking from thinkers' books the image-filled kernel, mistaking them for poets, in other words, or else he dug out science, philosophy, history from pondering over Abraham sacrificing Isaac, and Oedipus blinding himself, and King Lear losing his mind in the storm.

It was pointless now to open the Bible: he already knew the game he would start playing, with the book of Job, identifying the election watchers, chairman, priest, in the characters who gather around the plagued man, to convince him how to deal with the Eternal.

Rather, sticking to texts that, even if you're just leafing through them, always offer something that grips you, the Communist Amerigo Ormea took up Marx. And in the *Youthful Writings* he found the passage that goes:

. . . Man's universality appears, practically speaking, in that same universality that makes all nature man's *inorganic* body, both because nature is (1) an immediate means of subsistence, and because it is (2) the matter, the object, and the instrument of man's vital activity. Nature is man's *inorganic body* precisely because it is not his human body. To say man *lives* on nature means that nature is his *body,* with which he must constantly progress, in order not to die. . . .

Swiftly, he was convinced Marx could mean also this: once outside the society that makes men become things, the totality of things—nature and industry—becomes human, and even the handicapped man, the Cottolengo man (or, in the worst hypothesis, simply man), is restored to the rights of the human race as he makes use of this total body, this extension of his body: the richness of what exists (also "inorganic, spiritual nature," he read earlier, perhaps through a residue of Hegelianism, that is to say, reasoned nature, as in science and art), what has become finally a general object of human conscience and human life. Can it also mean that "Communism" (Amerigo tried to make the word sound as if it were being uttered for the first time, so that it would again be possible to think, beneath the noun's husk, of this dream of a death and resurrection of nature, a Utopia's treasure buried beneath the foundations of "scientific" doctrine), that Communism will restore sound legs to the lame, and eyesight to the blind? Will the lame man then have many, many legs at his disposal to run with, so many that he won't notice if one of his own is missing? That the blind man will have so many antennae to understand the world that he will forget he has no eyes?

The telephone rang. Lia asked: "Well, where have you been all morning?"

Amerigo had explained nothing to her, and he had no intention of doing so. Not for any special reason, but because there were some things he talked about with Lia, and some things he never mentioned; and this was one of the latter. "There's an election on, you know," was all he said.

"Voting takes two minutes. You just go and vote. I've already been."

(For whom she had voted was a question Amerigo didn't bother to ask himself, and to ask her would have cost him an effort, it meant mixing one kind of problem—his relationship with her—and another—his relationship with politics. However, this silence weighed on his conscience, both because of the party—every Communist's duty was to make "grass-roots" propaganda, and he didn't even try with his mistress!—and because of her; why did he never talk with her of the things that were most important to him?)

"Well, I was busy. I'm one of the men who sit behind the table at the polls," he said, feeling very annoyed.

"Ah. I only asked because I wanted to plan this afternoon."

"Nothing doing. I have to go back there."

"Again?"

"I've got myself involved." And he decided to add: "The party, you know . . ."

(Amerigo's being a Communist meant no more to Lia than if he were the fan of one football team or another. Was this right?)

"Why don't you find somebody else to take your place?"

"I told you: when you start, you have to stay to the end. It's the law."

"Smart, weren't you?"

"Hm."

She was expert in making him nervous, this girl.

"It's the last day of your week. Oh, you know. You remember, I told you? The week of your horoscope . . ."

"Lia, what's my horoscope got to do with . . ."

"A decisive week in your love life, other activities not advised."

"That magazine's horoscope!"

"It's the best; it's never wrong."

They began one of their usual arguments, caused by the fact that, instead of saying "Horoscopes are all lies," which would have been natural for him, Amerigo became involved —thanks to his habit of looking at things from the adversary's point of view and his aversion to expressing obvious notions—in a technical analysis of astrology, trying to prove to her that the very people who believed in the stars' influence should find it impossible to trust horoscopes in newspapers and magazines.

"No, listen: the birth hour isn't only distinguished by the position of the Sun but . . ."

"What do I care? For you and me, those horoscopes always hit the nail on the head!"

"You're irrational, Lia, you're always irrational." Amerigo was growing angry. "If you would just look at the planets with some logic. Take Pluto, which is supposed to . . ."

"I'm basing what I say on experience, not on talk," Lia answered furiously. There was no understanding each other.

After the phone call, Amerigo sat down at the table and began to eat, the book open before him, and at the same time he tried to resume his interrupted thinking. He had come to a point, an opening tiny as a pinprick, through which he could see a human world of a structure so different that even nature's injustices lost their importance, became negligible, and there was an end to that struggle for mastery which lies in charity, between those who offer it and those who receive it. . . . But no, he couldn't find his place again, it was hopeless, he had lost the thread; it was always the same with that girl! Just the sound of her voice seemed enough to alter all the proportions around him, so whatever he happened to argue about with Lia (anything at all, some piece of nonsense, horoscopes, Colonel Townsend, the best diet for colitis victims) became of all-consuming importance, and he was engulfed body and soul in a quarrel which then continued as a soliloquy, an inner rage, accompanying him for the rest of the day.

He realized that he had also lost his appetite.

"Irrational, that's what she is, that girl!" he repeated to himself, growing angry all over again, knowing, at the same time, Lia could be no other way and if she were some other way it would be as if she didn't exist. "Irrational, prelogical!"—and he felt a double pleasure, reviving his own suffering at Lia's way of thinking, and applying to it, cruelly, aggressively, the most elementary logic.

"Prelogical, prelogical!" In his imaginary argument, he went on flinging this word in Lia's face, and now he regretted not having said it to her: "Prelogical! You know what you are? You're prelogical!" And he would have wanted her to understand at once what he meant, or rather, no: he wanted her not to understand so he could explain to her at length what he meant by "prelogical" and so she would be offended and so he could go on calling her "prelogical" and, at the same time, explain to her clearly why she had no reason to be offended, on the contrary, why "prelogical" in her case was the right word for her, because when she heard herself called "prelogical" she was offended as if "prelogical" were an insult, whereas instead . . .

He threw down his napkin, rose from the table, and went to the telephone. He called her. He needed to quarrel again and to say "prelogical" to her, but even before he had said "Hello" Lia said in a low voice: "Sssh . . . be quiet. . . ."

Music was coming, muffled, from the other end of the wire. Amerigo had already lost his self-confidence. "Well . . . what is it?"

"Sssh . . ." Lia said, as if she didn't want to miss a note.

"What record is it?" Amerigo asked, just to be saying something.

"La-la-la . . . Can't you hear? I gave you the same one."

"Oh, of course . . ." Amerigo said; he didn't care. "Listen, I meant to tell you . . ."

"Sssh," Lia whispered, "I want to hear the end. . . ."

"You think I called you up to listen to a record over the phone? If that's what I wanted, I could listen to one of my own without getting up from the table!"

There was a silence at the other end of the wire; the flow of music had also stopped. Then Lia said, slowly: ". . . Ah. *Your own* records?"

Amerigo realized he had said the worst thing he could have said. He tried, swiftly, to remedy the situation: *"Mine* . . . I mean *yours,* the ones you've given me. . . ."

Too late. "Oh, I know . . . you don't care who gave them to you. . . ."

This was an old question, unbearable for Amerigo. He had certain records, so what? They meant nothing to him, but once, for some reason he had told Lia he never tired of listening to them; nothing wrong with that; but when Lia learned, from a thoughtless remark of his, that the records had been given to him by one Maria Pia, she had blown the thing up in such a disagreeable way that they could never talk about it afterward without quarreling. Then she had given him some new records; and she wanted him to throw away the old ones. Amerigo had said no, on principle; he didn't care about the records or about Maria Pia, that was all water under the bridge, but he wouldn't allow objective facts like the music on a record to be linked with subjective ones like his feelings for the person who had given him the record, nor would he admit that he had to explain why he wouldn't allow this connection: it was an intolerable business, and now it had trapped him once more.

He was in a hurry, but he couldn't cut her off without making matters worse. Especially since, this time, she was pretending to say the things he always said: "Oh, I understand, a piece of music is a piece of music, the memory of a person has nothing to do with it . . ." and he was trying to say the things that ought to please her: "But I listen to the records I like best, I mean the ones you picked out, don't I?" So he couldn't tell whether they were still quarreling or not.

And Lia at a certain point put the record back on, and hummed the tune along with it, and at a certain point, Amerigo, aside, that is to the maid asking if she could clear away, said: "Just a moment, I have to finish the soup!" and then Lia laughed and said: "But you're mad! Haven't you finished lunch yet?" And so they said good-by and there was no doubt that they had made peace.

The thought that preoccupied Amerigo during the main course was this: Hegel was the only one who had understood anything about love. He got up three times before finishing the dish in order to search among his books; but he had none of Hegel's works in the house, just a few books on Hegel or with chapters on Hegel, and for all his leafing through them between mouthfuls—"The Desire for Desire," "The Other," "Recognition"—he couldn't find the place.

The telephone rang. It was Lia again. "Listen, I have to talk to you. I made up my mind I wasn't going to tell you, but I will. No, not over the phone, it's not something to discuss on the phone. I'm not yet sure, really, I'll tell you about it when I'm sure, no, I'd better tell you now. It's something important. I'm afraid it's yes" (they spoke in clipped phrases: she, because she couldn't decide to be frank; he, because the maid was in the next room—at one point he went and shut the kitchen door—and also because he was afraid he understood), "no use getting angry, Amerigo darling, if you're angry, then you must have understood, well, I'm not a hundred per cent sure, but . . ." In other words, she was trying to tell him she was pregnant.

There was a chair near the telephone. Amerigo sat down. He didn't say anything, until Lia finally said: "Hello? Hello?" thinking they had been cut off.

At times like this Amerigo would have liked to remain calm, master of the situation—he wasn't a boy any longer! —to put up a reassuring front, a serene, protective presence, and at the same time be cold and lucid, the sort of man who knows what has to be done. Instead, he immediately lost his head. He felt his throat go dry, he couldn't speak calmly, or think before he spoke. "Oh no, you must be crazy, how can you . . ." and he was immediately in the grip of rage, a precipitous rage that seemed to want to drive back, into nonbeing, the glimpsed eventuality, the thought that permitted no other thought, the obligation to act, to assume responsibilities, to decide another's life and one's own. He went on talking, inveighing: "You tell me like this?

You're so irresponsible! How can you stay calm?" until he provoked her indignant, wounded reaction: "You're the irresponsible one. No, you're right: it was crazy of me to tell you. I shouldn't have said anything, I should have managed alone, and never seen you again!"

Amerigo knew well that he was calling her "irresponsible" because that was what he wanted to call himself, he was angry only with himself, but at that moment his regret and his guilt were translated into an aversion for the woman in trouble, for that risk that could become an irrevocable presence, that could make an endless future of what now seemed to him a relationship that had already lasted long enough, something finished, relegated to the past.

At the same time he felt constant remorse for his egoism, for having such a comfortable role compared to hers; and the girl's courage seemed great to him, sublime, and now his admiration of this courage, the fondness for her uncertainty, so linked to his own, and his certainty that he was after all better than his first hasty reaction made him seem, that he could draw on a reserve supply of mature judgment and responsibility—all this led him to assume a completely different attitude, again with precipitate haste, and say: "No, no, darling, don't worry, I'm here, I'm beside you, whatever happens. . . ."

Her voice melted quickly, seeking an expression of consolation. "Listen, after all, if . . ." And he was already fearing he had gone too far, perhaps making her think him prepared to have a child of hers, so without breaking off his protective pressure, he tried to clarify his intentions. "You'll see, darling, it'll be nothing. . . . I'll take care of everything, poor sweetheart, don't worry, in a few days' time you won't even remember . . ."

At which, from the other end of the wire, came a shrill,

almost strident voice: "What are you talking about? What are you going to take care of? What have you got to do with it? The child's mine. . . . If I want to have a baby, I'll have it! I'm not asking you for anything! I never want to see you again! My child will grow up without even knowing who you are!"

This didn't mean she really wanted to have the baby; perhaps she only wanted to release a woman's natural resentment against the facility with which a man does and undoes; but she redoubled Amerigo's alarm, and he protested: "No, no, you can't . . . it isn't right to have children like that, it's not being responsible . . ." until she hung up as he was in mid-sentence.

"I've finished, you can wash up," he said to the maid. He went back and sat down by the bookcase and thought of when he had been seated there earlier, as if it were a remote time, serene, carefree. Most of all, he felt humiliated. For him, procreation represented, first of all, a defeat of his ideas. Amerigo was an ardent supporter of birth control, even though his party's attitude on the subject was either agnostic or hostile. Nothing shocked him so much as the ease with which people multiply, and the more hungry and backward, the more they keep having children, not so much because they want them as because they are accustomed to letting nature take its course, accustomed to carelessness and neglect. But to maintain this show of detached bitterness and amazement, like some Scandinavian Social Democrat, toward the underdeveloped world, he had to keep himself blameless of that sin. . . .

Now, too, the hours spent at Cottolengo began to weigh on him, all that India of people born to unhappiness, that silent question, an accusation of all those who procreate. This sight, this awareness, he thought, would not be without consequences as if he were the pregnant mother, sensitive as a photographic plate, or as if atomic disintegration were already at work inside him and he could produce only disastrous progeny.

How could he return to reading now, to universal reflections? Even the books open before him were his enemies: the Bible with that eternal problem of continuing, amid famines and deserts, the generations of a human race that wishes to save every drop of its seed, still unsure of its survival; and Marx, who also wanted no limitation of human semination, convinced of the earth's infinite richness: forward, all was flowing fecundity, go on, hurrah! Both books were great counselors! How could anyone not understand that the danger to the human race now was quite the opposite?

It was late; they would be waiting for him at the polls; the others had to take their turn; he should hurry. But first he called Lia once more, though he still didn't know what to say to her: "Lia, listen, I have to go out now, but look here, I . . ."

"Sssh . . ." she said: the record was playing again as if that middle telephone call hadn't existed, and Amerigo felt a spurt of annoyance ("There, for her it's nothing, for her it's nature, for her the logic of the mind doesn't count, only the logic of physiology!") and also a kind of reassurance, because Lia was really the same Lia as always: "Hush . . . you must listen to it to the end. . . ." And, after all, what could have changed in her? Not much: something still nonexistent, which could therefore be thrust back into nothingness (at what point does a being become a being?), a mere biological potentiality, blind (at what point does a human become human?), a something that only a deliberate desire to make human could add to the ranks of human presences.

XII

A CERTAIN number of the voters registered at Cottolengo were patients who couldn't leave their beds or their wards. For such cases the law provides that some of the election watchers be chosen to set up a "detachment" of the polls which can go and collect the votes of the sick in their "place of treatment," in other words, on the spot. They agreed to form this "detachment" with the chairman, the clerk, the woman in white, and Amerigo. They were issued two boxes, one with the blank ballots and the other to contain the ballots after they had been marked. They were also given a special folder, the register, and a list of the "voters in place of treatment."

They gathered up these things and went off. They were led up some stairs by a young man, one of the "bright" ones, tiny and squat, who, despite his ugly features, his shaved head, and the thick eyebrows which grew together, proved up to his task and full of concern; he almost seemed to have landed in there by mistake, because of his looks. "In this wing there are four." They went in.

It was a huge, long room, and they passed between two white rows of beds. Coming from the darkness of the stairs, they were dazzled, painfully, in perhaps what was only a sensation of defense, a kind of refusal to perceive in the white mounds of sheets and pillows the human-colored shapes that rose from them; or else it was a first translation, from hearing to sight, of a shrill, constant animal cry: geee . . . geee . . . geee . . . which rose from some part of the ward, answered at times from another point by a chuckling or barking animal sound: gaa! gaa! gaa! gaa!

The shrill cry came from a tiny red face, all eyes, the

mouth opened in motionless laughter: a boy, sitting in bed in a white shirt, or rather not sitting, but emerging, trunk and head, from the bed's opening as a plant peeps up in a pot, like a plant's stalk that ended (there was no sign of arms) in that fishlike head, and this boy-plant-fish (At what point can a human being be called human? Amerigo asked himself) moved up and down, bending forward at each "geee . . . gee . . ." And the "gaa! gaa!" that answered him came from another boy who seemed even more shapeless, though a head stuck out in his bed, greedy, flushed, a large mouth, and it must have had arms—or fins—which moved beneath the sheets where it seemed sheathed (to what degree can a creature be called a creature of whatever species?), and other voices echoed, making more sounds, excited perhaps by the appearance of people in the ward, and there was also a panting and moaning, like a shout ready to burst forth but promptly stifled. This came from an adult.

In that wing, some were adults—it seemed—and some, boys and children, if one was to judge by the dimensions and by signs like the hair or the skin color, which count among people outside. One was a giant, with a huge infant's head held erect by pillows: he lay immobile, his arms hidden behind his back, the chin on the chest which extended into an obese belly, the eyes looked at nothing, the gray hair hung over the huge forehead (an elderly creature, who had survived in that long fetus-growth?), frozen in a dazed sadness.

The priest, the one with the beret, was already in the ward, waiting for them, he, too, with his list in hand. Seeing Amerigo, he glowered. But at that moment Amerigo was no longer thinking of the senseless reason for his being there; he felt the boundary line he was supposed to check was now another: not that of the "people's will," long since lost from sight, but the boundary of the human.

The priest and the chairman had approached the Reverend Mother who was in charge of that wing, with the names of the four registered voters. The nun pointed them out. Other nuns came forward, carrying a screen, a little table, all the things necessary to the voting in there.

One bed at the end of the ward was empty, neatly made; its occupant, perhaps already convalescing, was sitting on a chair beside the bed, dressed in flannel pajamas with a jacket over them, and sitting at the opposite side of the bed was an old man wearing a hat, certainly the patient's father, who had come to visit him that Sunday. The son was young, simple-minded, of normal stature but somehow, it seemed, numbed in his movements. The father cracked some almonds for the son and passed them to him across the bed, and the son took them and slowly put them to his mouth. And the father watched him chew.

The fish-boys burst out with their cries and every so often the Reverend Mother broke away from the polling group to go and quiet one who had become overexcited, but without much success. Each thing that happened in the ward was separate from the other things, as if each bed enclosed a world out of communication with the rest, except for the cries that stimulated one another, in a crescendo, and spread a general agitation, partly like the racket of sparrows, and partly mournful, moaning. Only the man with the enormous head was immobile, as if untouched by any sound.

Amerigo went on watching the father and son. The son had long limbs and a long face, which was also hairy and numb, perhaps half blocked by paralysis. The father was a peasant, also in his best suit, and in some ways, especially in the length of his face and his hands, he resembled his son. Not in the eyes: the son had the helpless eyes of an animal, while the father's eyes were half shut, wary, the eyes of an old farmer. They were sitting obliquely on their chairs, at either side of the bed, so they could stare at each other, and they paid no attention to anything around them. Amerigo kept his gaze on them, perhaps to rest from (or to avoid) other sights, or perhaps, even more, because he was somehow fascinated.

Meanwhile the other officials were taking the vote of someone in bed. They did it like this: they put the screen around him, with the table behind it, and, as he was a paralytic, the nun voted for him. They removed the screen, Amerigo looked at him: a purple face, flung back as if dead, mouth gaping, gums bared, eyes wide. Only that face, sunk in the pillow, could be seen: it was hard as a stick, except for a gasping that seemed to whistle at the base of his throat.

Where do they get the nerve to have such creatures vote? Amerigo asked himself, and only then did he remember that it was his job to prevent them.

They were already setting up the screen at another bed. Amerigo followed them. Another hairless, swollen face, stiff, with opened, twisted mouth, the eyeballs sticking out of the lids without lashes. But this inmate was restless, disturbed.

"But there's a mistake!" Amerigo said. "How can this man vote?"

"There's his name: Morin, Giuseppe," the chairman said. Then, to the priest: "This is the one?"

"Yes, here's the certificate," the priest said. "Motor impediment of the limbs. You're going to assist him, Reverend Mother, aren't you?"

"Oh yes, yes, poor Giuseppe," the nun said.

58

The man in the bed jerked as if he were being given electric shocks, groaning.

It was up to Amerigo now. He tore himself forcibly from his thoughts, from that barely glimpsed, remote frontier territory—frontier between what and what?—and everything on this or that side of it seemed mist.

"Just a moment," he said in an expressionless voice, knowing he was repeating a formula, talking in a void. "Is the voter capable of recognizing the person who is voting for him? Is he capable of expressing his wishes? Signor Morin, I'm speaking to you: are you able to do this?"

"Here we go again," the priest said to the chairman. "Reverend Mother is with them day and night here, and they ask him if he knows her. . . ." He shook his head, with a little laugh.

Reverend Mother also smiled, but her smile was for all and for no reason. The problem of being recognized, Amerigo thought, didn't exist for her; and he was impelled to compare the old nun's gaze with that of the peasant spending Sunday at Cottolengo to stare into the eyes of his idiot son. The nun didn't need recognition from those she helped, the good she derived from them—in exchange for the good she did them—was a general good, of which nothing was lost. Instead, the old peasant stared into his son's eyes to be recognized, to keep from losing him, from losing that little, poor thing that was his, his son.

When no sign of recognition came from that trunk of a man with a voter's certificate, the Reverend Mother was the least concerned of all: and yet she bustled about, carrying out the election formality as one of the many formalities the outside world demanded which, for reasons she didn't bother to investigate, affected the efficiency of her service; and so she tried to raise that body's shoulders on the pillows, as if it could make a pretense of sitting up. But no position suited that body any more: the arms, in the great white shirt, were numbed, the hands were bent back, and so were the legs, as if the limbs were trying to turn upon themselves, seeking refuge.

"Can't he speak?" the chairman asked, raising one finger, as if apologizing for his doubt. "Can't he speak at all?"

"No, Mr. Chairman, he can't," the priest said. "Hey, can you speak? No? You can't? You see: he can't speak. But he understands. You know who she is, don't you? She's good, isn't she? Yes? He understands. For that matter, he voted in the last election."

"Oh, yes," the Reverend Mother said, "this one has always voted."

"He's in that condition, but he can understand . . ." the woman in white said then, in a tone that might have been a question, an affirmation, or a hope. And she addressed the nun, as if to involve her too in this question-affirmation-hope: "He understands, doesn't he?"

"Ah, well . . ." the Reverend Mother held out her arms and raised her eyes.

"Enough of this farce," Amerigo said. "He's unable to express his wishes, and so he can't vote. Is that clear? We must show some respect. Nothing more need be said."

(Did he mean "some respect" toward the election or "some respect" toward the suffering flesh? He didn't specify.)

He expected his words to start a battle. But instead, nothing happened. Nobody protested. With a sigh, shaking his head, he looked at the twisted man. "True, he's been getting worse," the priest agreed, in a low voice. "He could still vote, even two years ago."

The chairman indicated the register to Amerigo. "What

do we do? Leave a blank, or shall we write a report separately?"

"Skip it, skip it," was all Amerigo could say; he was thinking of another question: Was it more humane to help them live or help them die? But he had no answer to that question either.

So he had won his battle: the paralytic's vote hadn't been extorted from him. But a vote: what did a vote matter? This was the argument Cottolengo kept repeating to him, with its moans and its cries: you see what a joke your will of the people becomes, nobody believes in it here, here they take their revenge on the secular powers, it would have been better to let even that vote go by, it would have been better if the part of power gained by such means were to be left ineradicable, inseparable from their authority, that they should assume and bear it forever.

"What about number 27? And number 15?" the Reverend Mother asked. "Are the others who were supposed to vote going to vote, then?"

After a glance at the list, the priest had gone over to one bed. He came back, shaking his head. "That one's in a bad way, too."

"He can't recognize anyone?" the woman supervisor asked, as if inquiring about a relative.

"He's got worse, much worse," the priest said. "We'll leave it at that."

"Then we'll cross this one off, too," the chairman said. "What about the fourth? Where is the fourth?"

But the priest had caught on by now, he only wanted to cut matters short. "If one can't vote, then the others can't either. Let's go . . ." and he took the chairman's arm, to urge him out, as the old man was trying to check the numbers on the beds. At a certain moment the chairman stopped at the motionless giant with the huge head, and consulted the list as if to verify that it was the fourth voter's number, but the priest pushed him away. "Come, let's go out. I can see that they've all got worse in here. . . ."

"The other years they had them do it," the nun said, as if she were talking of injections.

"Well, now they're worse," the priest concluded. "Obviously, a sick person either gets well or he gets worse."

"Not all of them are capable of voting, of course, poor things," the woman in white said, as if apologizing.

"Oh, my goodness!" the nun laughed. "There are some that can't vote, all right. You should see over there, on the veranda. . . ."

"Can we see?" the woman in white asked.

"Why, of course, come this way." The nun opened the glass door.

"If they're the kind that frighten people, I'm afraid," the clerk said. Amerigo, too, had drawn back.

The Reverend Mother was still smiling: "No, no, why be afraid? They're good creatures. . . ."

The door opened on a terrace, a kind of veranda; and there was a semicircle of huge high chairs, with a number of young men seated in them, their heads shaved, but not their faces, their hands resting on the chair arms. They wore blue-striped robes which fell to the ground, hiding the pot beneath each chair, but the stink and the trickles of the overflow were visible on the floor, between their bare legs, their feet in clogs. They too had the same fraternal resemblance that reigned at Cottolengo and their expressions were the same, with their shapeless, snaggle-toothed mouths open in a snigger that could also be a kind of weeping; and the racket they made was a single, lifeless bleat of laughter and tears. Standing in front of them, an assistant—one of those ugly but brighter boys—kept order, with a switch in his hand, and he intervened when one of the boys wanted to touch himself, or get up, or when he disturbed the others or made too much noise. A bit of sun shone against the glass panes of the veranda, and the young men laughed at the reflections, then passed abruptly to wrath, shouting at one another, then they immediately forgot.

The election watchers looked in for a moment, from the door, then drew back, and went along the ward. The Reverend Mother preceded them. "You're a saint," the woman in white said. "If there weren't souls like you, these poor unhappy things . . ."

The old nun looked around, with her limpid, happy eyes, as if she were in a garden filled with health, and she answered the other's praise with those ready-made remarks that express modesty and love of one's neighbor, but her words were natural, because everything must have been very natural for her, there must have been no doubts, since she had chosen definitively to live for these inmates.

Amerigo, too, would have liked to express his admiration and fondness to her, but what occurred to him was a speech on how society should be, according to him, a society where a woman like her would no longer be considered a saint, because persons like her would be countless, instead of being relegated to the margin of society, shut off in their halo of sanctity; and living, as she did, for a universal goal would be more natural than living for any special goal, and it would be possible for each to express himself, his own, buried, secret, individual energy, in his social functions, in his personal relationship with the common good. . . .

But the more he stubbornly thought these things, the more he realized that this, too, wasn't what mattered to him at that moment: it was something else, for which he couldn't find words. In short, facing the old nun, he still felt himself in his own world, confirmed in the moral feelings he had always (though inaccurately and with effort) tried to base his life on, but the thought that gnawed at him there in the ward was another, it was still the presence of that peasant and his son, who indicated to him a territory he didn't know.

The nun had chosen this ward freely, she had totally identified herself—rejecting the rest of the world—in that mission or militancy, and yet—or rather for that very reason—she remained distinct from the object of her mission, mistress of herself, happily free. The old peasant, instead, had chosen nothing, the tie that bound him to the ward was not something he had wanted, his life was elsewhere, on his land, but he made this Sunday journey to watch his son chew.

Now that the young idiot had finished his slow treat, father and son, still sitting at the sides of the bed, kept their hands on their knees, hands heavy with bones and veins, and their heads were twisted—the father's under his pulled-down hat, and the son's shaved like a convict's—so they could still see each other out of the corner of an eye.

"There," Amerigo thought, "those two, as they are, are necessary to each other."

And he thought: "There, this way of being is love."

And then: "Humanity reaches as far as love reaches; it has no frontiers except those we give it."

XIII

IT WAS growing dark. The "detachment" went on through the wards: the women's wards now. The job of collecting votes from those beds, with the screens to be moved each time, seemed endless. These patients, these old women, sometimes took ten minutes, a quarter of an hour. "Have you finished, Signora? Can we collect the ballot?" The poor woman, behind the screen, might even be in her death agony. "Have you folded the ballot? You have?" They took away the screen: the ballot was still there, open, white; or else with a squiggle, a scrawl.

Amerigo was vigilant; the patient had to be left alone behind the screen; the business of failing eyesight or paralyzed hands was no longer tolerated; there was no further talk even of allowing the nun to make the "x"; Amerigo was inflexible: if the voter couldn't vote by himself, too bad, then he just wouldn't vote.

From the moment when he began to feel less alien to those poor creatures, the rigor of his political task had also become less alien to him. It was as if, in that first ward, the net of objective contradictions that held him in a kind of resignation to the worst had been broken, and now he felt lucid, as if everything were clear to him, as if he understood what should be demanded of society and what, on the other hand, couldn't be asked of society; but you had to achieve this awareness in person, otherwise it was useless.

Everyone knows those moments when you seem to understand everything; perhaps the next moment you try to define what you've understood and it all vanishes. Perhaps nothing had changed very much in him; his actions and their motives, his self-defense and so on—it's hard for that to change. You can talk about it all you like, but after a certain point a man is what he is.

However, what he thought he had finally come to understand was his relationship with Lia, and among those beds that seemed to conceal in a vague penumbra all the evil that can disfigure women's bodies (he was in a central room that branched out in broad-vaulted wards, dimly lighted by the reflection of shaded bulbs against the whiteness of the sheets —contracted arms rested there, like red or yellow branches —and these vaults or wings converged on a column, at whose foot, from one bed, a constant, squeaking cry was raised, from a bonneted form that must have been—he didn't want to look—a child, but reduced to the mere pulse of that cry, and everything around it—the scene and the shadows that rose from the pillows—seemed to exist only because of that single, infantile effort to live, and the chorus of moans and gasping from all the beds seemed to come to support that voice that was as if bodiless), Amerigo saw Lia, but it was the sadness of Lia's gray eyes that he saw, the hint of flight at the back of the eyes that couldn't be driven out or consoled, the meek way her hair had of falling over her soft shoulders, but with the quality of a crouching, wild creature that wriggles free the moment you touch it, and the helpless way in which the tip of her breast rose above her arm: everything about her demanded protection, pity, but you couldn't communicate it to her, because at the moment when you thought you had, she would roll over with a little laugh of defiance, her gray, hostile glance darkening, the flow of her hair stretching down her back to the swelling of her hips, and the long leg advancing with a light step as if she were shrugging off her burden of before. But now this daydream of Lia, this love seen as reciprocal and constant challenge or corrida or safari, no longer seemed to him in contrast to those hospital shades: they were strings of the same knot or tangle in which—often (or always) painfully —people are tied together. In fact, for the space of a second (that is to say, forever) he thought he had understood how the same meaning of the word "love" could comprehend a thing like his affair with Lia and the peasant's silent Sunday visit to his son at Cottolengo.

He was so excited by this discovery that he couldn't wait to discuss it with Lia, and when he saw the open door of an office he asked a nun if he might telephone. Lia's number was busy. "I'll try again later, may I? Thank you." And he began to shift back and forth between the "detachment," which moved among the wards, and the telephone which always gave the busy signal, and he was less and less sure of what he wanted to say to Lia; now he would like to explain everything to her, the election, Cottolengo, the people he had seen there, but there was a nun who came and went in that office and he wouldn't be able to talk for long. And every time he heard the busy signal, he felt both irritation and relief, also because he was afraid the conversation would turn to that certain problem, and he didn't want to face it: or rather, he wanted only to tell her that—while he hadn't changed his intentions—even in weighing those intentions he was a different person.

So, though he was now hoping the girl's number would go on being busy, he didn't stop calling her, and when all of a sudden it was free, he started talking to her about something quite different, about the fact that her line was always busy.

She answered with remarks equally far from the point, that everything between the two of them was as always, but for Amerigo what was as always now seemed heartbreaking and filled with emotion, and he couldn't even pay attention to her words, but only to their sound, as if it were a kind of music.

Suddenly he pricked up his ears. Lia was saying: "And besides, I don't know what to take with me, perhaps I should pack a light overcoat. What will the weather be like now, in Liverpool?"

"What? You're not going to Liverpool?"

"Of course, I am. Tomorrow. I'm leaving tomorrow."

"What are you talking about? Why?" Amerigo was alarmed by what a journey to Liverpool might mean, but also reassured because her leaving dismissed their earlier fears, and confused because Lia always made the most unexpected decisions, and heartened because Lia was still the same Lia.

"You know: I have to go visit my aunt in Liverpool."

"But you said you weren't going."

"But you told me to go, you said it yourself: go."

"I? When?"

"Yesterday."

It was the same old story. "Uff. Maybe I said 'go to Liverpool,' but I was just talking. It was like saying: go to the devil, don't bother me with this business of Liverpool and your aunt. If I said: 'Well, *go* to Liverpool,' it didn't mean you were to go there!"

He grew angry, but he knew that, with Lia, love was precisely this way of growing angry with her.

"But you told me to go!"

"You're like that man who took everything literally!"

Lia replied, resentfully: "What man? Whom are you talking about? What do you mean?" as if in Amerigo's words she had sensed something extremely offensive; and Amerigo no longer knew how to end the conversation, and he was full of irritation and fury, and at the same time he knew he was caught and hanging up the phone was meaningless.

XIV

THE LAST votes they had to collect were from some nuns confined to their beds. The watchers advanced through long corridors, among rows of testers with white curtains draped up over some of the beds to frame an aged nun leaning on the pillows, emerging from the covers, fully dressed, even to the freshly starched wing of her coif. The conventual architecture (probably dating from the middle of the last century, but virtually timeless), the décor, the nuns' habits, offered a sight that must have been exactly the same in a convent of the seventeenth century. Amerigo was certainly setting foot in a place of this sort for the first time. And in such cases, a character like him—what with the historical fascination, aesthetism, the recollection of famous books, his interest (typical of revolutionaries) in how institutions shape the aspect and the spirit of civilizations—was capable of giving way to a sudden enthusiasm for the nuns' dormitory, of allowing himself almost to feel envy, in the name of future societies, of an image that, like this row of white testers, contained so many things: practicality, repression, serenity, command, exactness, absurdity.

But no, not at all. He had passed through a world that rejected form, and now, finding himself in this harmony virtually removed from the world, he realized it didn't matter to him. There was something else, now, that he was trying to hold in his gaze, not images of the past and the future. The past (for the very fact that its image was complete and no change could be thought of: like this dormitory) seemed to him a huge snare. And the future, when one imagines it (that is, when one connects it with the past), also turns into a snare.

Here the voting proceeded more swiftly. The ballots were placed on a tray, over the knees of the nun, sitting up in her bed; the white curtains of the tester were drawn. "Have you voted, sister?" The curtains were drawn back again, the ballots were put in the ballot box. The huge bed was occupied by a mountain of pillows and by the body of the old woman, under her great white pectoral, with the wings of her coif touching the sky of the canopy. Waiting there, outside the curtain, the chairman, the clerk, and the watchers seemed smaller.

We're like Little Red Ridinghood visiting her sick grandmother, Amerigo thought. Perhaps, when we open the curtains, we won't find Granny any more, but the wolf instead. And then: Every sick granny is always a wolf.

XV

THEY WERE together again, all the election officials in the big room. There wasn't much of a crowd now: the names that hadn't been ticked off, in the list of registered voters, were very few. The chairman, his nervous tension past, exuded, as a reaction, an equally erratic joviality. "Ah, tomorrow, the final tally, and then the election's over! After that, ladies and gentlemen, our duty's done! So for another four years at least we don't have to think about it!"

"We'll start thinking about it, all right . . ." Amerigo grumbled, already foreseeing (though he was mistaken) that the day he was living through would be remembered among the dates of an Italian reaction (instead, the famous "swindle law" didn't pass, Italy went on, expressing more and more clearly its two-headed nature), the date of a worldwide petrification (but throughout the world the things that seem most stony really move), pacifying only lazy consciences like the chairman of these polls, and stifling the aroused consciences' need to seek further (instead, everything proved more and more complex, and it was increasingly difficult to distinguish the positive and the negative thing, and increasingly necessary to discard appearances and look for the essences that weren't makeshift: few and still uncertain . . .).

Now the watchers gathered around one of the last voters, a big man with a cap. He had no hands; he had been like this since birth: two cylindrical stumps came from his sleeves, but, pressing one against the other, he could hold and handle objects, even small ones (the pencil, a sheet of paper: in fact, he had voted by himself, had folded the ballot by himself), as if in the grip of two huge fingers. "Anything: even light a cigarette," the man said, and with rapid movements he extracted the pack from his pocket, held it to his mouth, drew out the cigarette, pressed the box of matches under his armpit, struck one, puffed on the cigarette, impassively.

They were all around him, asking him how he did it, how he had learned. The man answered curtly; he had the large, flushed face of a worker, steady, without expression. "I know how to do everything," he said. "I'm fifty years old. I grew up in Cottolengo." He spoke with his chin jutting forward, with a hard, almost defiant manner. Amerigo thought: Man triumphs even over malign biological mutations; and he recognized in the man's features, in his clothes and manner, the traits that mark working humanity, also deprived—symbolically and literally—of something of its completeness, and yet able to build itself, to affirm the decisive role of *homo faber*.

"I know how to do any kind of job by myself," the big

man in the cap was saying. "The nuns taught me. Here at Cottolengo we do everything for ourselves. Workshops and everything. We're like a city. I've always lived in Cottolengo. We don't lack for anything. The nuns see to it we have everything."

He was confident and impenetrable: in that sort of smugness at his strength, his belonging to an order that had made of him what he was. Will the city that can multiply man's hands, Amerigo asked himself, be already the city of the whole man? Or is *homo faber* valid because he never considers his wholeness sufficiently achieved?

"You're fond of them, aren't you, of the nuns?" the woman in the white blouse asked him now, eager to hear a consoling word at the end of the day.

The man went on repeating in a sharp, almost hostile tone, like the dutiful citizen of the productive civilizations (Amerigo was thinking of both the great countries): "Thanks to the nuns, I was able to learn. Without the nuns to help me, I wouldn't be anything. Now I can do whatever I want. You can't say a thing against the nuns. There's nobody like the nuns. . . ."

Homo faber's city, Amerigo thought, always runs the risk of mistaking its institutions for the secret fire without which cities are not founded and machinery's wheels aren't set in motion; and in defending institutions, unawares, you can let the fire die out.

He went to the window. A shred of sunset glowed among the sad buildings. The sun was already down but there was a reddish color behind the outline of the rooftops and the eaves, and in the courtyards it opened perspectives of a city that had never been seen.

Women, dwarfs, passed by in the yard, pushing a wheelbarrow of twigs. It was a heavy load. Another woman, huge, a giantess, came and pushed it, almost running, and she laughed. They all laughed. Another woman, also huge, walked in sweeping, with a twig broom. A very fat woman was pushing a kind of caldron between high poles, on bicycle wheels, perhaps the evening soup. Even the ultimate city of imperfection has its perfect hour, the watcher thought, the hour, the moment, when every city is the City.

Smog

Translated by William Weaver

THAT WAS a time when I didn't give a damn about anything, the period when I came to settle in this city. Settle is the wrong term. I had no desire to be settled in any sense; I wanted everything around me to remain flowing, temporary, because I felt it was the only way to save my inner stability, though what that consisted of, I couldn't have said. So when, after a whole series of recommendations, I was offered the job as managing editor of the magazine *Purification*, I came here to the city and looked for a place to live.

To a young man who has just got off the train, the city—as everyone must know—seems like one big station: no matter how much he walks about, the streets are still squalid, garages, warehouses, cafés with zinc counters, trucks discharging stinking gas in his face, as he constantly shifts his suitcase from hand to hand, as he feels his hands swell and become dirty, his underwear stick to him, his nerves grow taut, and everything he sees is nerve-racking, piecemeal. I found a suitable furnished room in one of those very streets; beside the door of the building there were two clusters of signs, bits of shoebox hung there on lengths of string, with the information that a room was for rent written in a rough hand, the tax stamps stuck in one corner. As I stopped to shift the suitcase again, I saw the signs and went into the building. At each stairway, on each landing there were a couple of ladies who rented rooms. I rang the bell on the second floor, stairway C.

The room was commonplace, a bit dark, because it opened on a courtyard, through a French window; that was how I was to come in, along a landing with a rusty railing. The room, in other words, was independent of the rest of the apartment, but to reach it I had to unlock a series of gates; the landlady, Signorina Margariti, was deaf and rightly feared thieves. There was no bath; the toilet was off the landing, in a kind of wooden shed; in the room there was a basin with running water, with no hot-water heater. But, after all, what could I expect? The price was right, or rather, it was the only possible price, because I couldn't spend more and I couldn't hope to find anything cheaper; besides, it was only temporary and I wanted to make that quite clear to myself.

"Yes, all right, I'll take it," I said to Signorina Margariti, who thought I had asked if the room was cold; she showed me the stove. With that, I had seen everything and I wanted to leave my luggage there and go out. But first I went to the basin and put my hands under the faucet; ever since I had arrived I had been anxious to wash them, but I only rinsed them hastily because I didn't feel like opening my suitcase to look for my soap.

"Oh, why didn't you tell me? I'll bring a towel right away!" Signorina Margariti said; she ran into the other room and came back with a freshly ironed towel which she placed on the footboard of the bed. I dashed a little water on my face, to freshen up—I felt irritatingly unclean—then I rubbed my face with the towel. That act finally made the landlady realize I meant to take the room. "Ah, you're going to take it! Good. You must want to change, to unpack; make yourself right at home, here's the wardrobe, give me your overcoat!"

I didn't let her slip the overcoat off my back; I wanted to go out at once. My only immediate need, as I tried to tell her, was some shelves; I was expecting a case of books, the little library I had managed to keep together in my haphazard life. It cost me some effort to make the deaf woman understand; finally she led me into the other rooms, her part of the house, to a little étagère, where she kept her work baskets and embroidery patterns; she told me she would clear it and put it in my room. I went out.

Purification was the organ of an Institute, where I was to report, to learn my duties. A new job, an unfamiliar city— had I been younger or had I expected more of life, these would have pleased and stimulated me; but not now, now I could see only the grayness, the poverty that surrounded me, and I could only plunge into it as if I actually liked it, because it confirmed my belief that life could be nothing else. I purposely chose to walk in the most narrow, anonymous, unimportant streets, though I could easily have gone along those with fashionable shopwindows and smart cafés; but I didn't want to miss the careworn expression on the faces of the passers-by, the shabby look of the cheap restaurants, the stagnant little stores, and even certain sounds which belong to narrow streets: the streetcars, the braking of pickup trucks, the sizzling of welders in the little workshops in the courtyards: all because that wear, that exterior clashing kept me from attaching too much importance to the wear, the clash that I carried within myself.

But to reach the Institute, I was obliged at one point to enter an entirely different neighborhood, elegant, shaded, old-fashioned, its side streets almost free of vehicles, and its main avenues so spacious that traffic could flow past without noise or jams. It was autumn; some of the trees were golden. The sidewalk did not flank walls, buildings, but fences with hedges beyond them, flower beds, gravel walks, constructions that lay somewhere between the palazzo and the villa, ornate in their architecture. Now I felt lost in a different way, because I could no longer find, as I had done before, things in which I recognized myself, in which I could read the future. (Not that I believe in signs, but when you're nervous, in a new place, everything you see is a sign.)

So I was a bit disoriented when I entered the Institute offices, different from the way I had imagined them, because they were the salons of an aristocratic palazzo, with mirrors and consoles and marble fireplaces and hangings and carpets (though the actual furniture was the usual kind for a modern office, and the lighting was the latest sort, with neon tubes). In other words, I was embarrassed then at having taken such an ugly, dark room, especially when I was led into the office of the president, Commendatore Cordà, who promptly greeted me with exaggerated expansiveness, treating me as an equal not only in social and business importance—which in itself was a hard position for me to maintain—but also as his equal in knowledge and interest in the problems which concerned the Institute and *Purification*. To tell the truth, I had believed it was all some kind of trick, something to mention with a wink; I had accepted the job just as a last resort, and now I had to act as if I had never thought of anything else in my whole life.

Commendatore Cordà was a man of about fifty, youthful in appearance, with a black mustache, a member of that generation, in other words, who despite everything still look youthful and wear a black mustache, the kind of man with whom I have absolutely nothing in common. Everything about him, his talk, his appearance—he wore an impeccable gray suit and a dazzlingly white shirt—his gestures—he moved one hand with his cigarette between his fingers— suggested efficiency, ease, optimism, broad-mindedness. He showed me the numbers of *Purification* that had appeared so far, put out by himself (who was its editor-in-chief) and the Institute's press officer, Signor Avandero (he introduced me to him; one of those characters who talk as if their words were typewritten). There were only a few, very skimpy issues, and you could see that they weren't the work of professionals. With the little I knew about magazines, I found a way to tell him—making no criticisms, obviously—how I would do it, the typographical changes I would make. I fell in with his tone, practical, confident in results; and I was pleased to see that we understood each other. Pleased, because the more efficient and optimistic I acted, the more I thought of that wretched furnished room, those squalid streets, that sense of rust and slime I felt on my skin, my not caring a damn about anything, and I seemed to be performing a trick, to be transforming, before the very eyes of Commendatore Cordà and Signor Avandero, all their technical-industrial efficiency into a pile of crumbs, and they were unaware of it, and Cordà kept nodding enthusiastically.

"Fine. Yes, absolutely, tomorrow, you and I agree, and meanwhile," Cordà said to me, "just to bring you up to date . . ." And he insisted on giving me the Proceedings of their latest convention to read. "Here," he took me over to some shelves where the mimeographed copies of all the speeches were arranged in so many stacks. "You see? Take this one, and this other one. Do you already have this? Here, count them and see if they're all there." And as he spoke, he picked up those papers and at that moment I noticed how they raised a little cloud of dust, and I saw the prints of his fingers outlined on their surface, which he had barely touched. Now the Commendatore, in picking up those papers, tried to give them a little shake, but just a slight one, as if he didn't want to admit they were dusty, and he also blew on them gently. He was careful not to put his fingers on the first page of each speech, but if he just grazed one with the tip of a fingernail, he left a little white streak over what seemed a gray background, since the paper was covered with a very fine veil of dust. Nevertheless, his fingers obviously became soiled, and he tried to clean them by bending the tips to his palm and rubbing them, but he only dirtied his whole hand with dust. Then instinctively he dropped his hands to the sides of his gray flannel trousers, caught himself just in time, raised them again, and so we both stood there, our fingertips in mid-air, handing speeches back and forth, taking them delicately by the margins as if they were nettle leaves, and meanwhile we went on smiling, nodding smugly, and saying: "Oh yes, a very interesting convention! Oh yes, an excellent endeavor!" but I noticed that the Commendatore became more and more nervous and insecure, and he couldn't look into my triumphant eyes, into my triumphant and desperate gaze, desperate because everything confirmed the fact that it was all exactly as I had believed it would be.

IT TOOK me some time to fall asleep. The room, which had seemed so quiet, at night filled with sounds that I learned, gradually, to decipher. Sometimes I could hear a voice distorted by a loud-speaker, giving brief, incomprehensible commands; if I had dozed off, I would wake up, thinking I was in a train, because the timbre and the cadence were those of the station loud-speakers, as during the night they rise to the surface of the traveler's restless sleep. When my ear had become accustomed to them, I managed to grasp the words: "Two ravioli with tomato sauce . . ." the voice said. "Grilled steak . . . Lamb chop . . ." My room was over the kitchen of the "Urbano Rattazzi" beer hall, which served hot meals even after midnight: from the counter, the waiters transmitted the orders to the cooks, snapping out the words over an intercom. In the wake of those messages, a confused sound of voices came up to me and, at times, the harmonizing chorus of a party. But it was a good place to eat in, somewhat expensive, with a clientele that was not vulgar: the nights were rare when some drunk cut up and overturned tables laden with glasses. As I lay in bed, the sounds of others' wakefulness reached me, muffled, without gusto or color, as if through a fog; the voice over the loud-speaker—"Side dish of French fries . . . Where's that ravioli?"—had a nasal, resigned melancholy.

At about half past two the "Urbano Rattazzi" beer hall pulled down its metal blinds; the waiters, turning up the collars of their topcoats over the Tyrolean jackets of their uniform, came out of the kitchen door and crossed the courtyard, chatting. At about three a metallic clanking invaded the courtyard: the kitchen workers were dragging out the heavy, empty beer drums, tipping them on their rims and rolling them along, banging one against the other; then the men began rinsing them out. They took their time, since they were no doubt paid by the hour; and they worked carelessly, whistling and making a great racket with those zinc drums, for a couple of hours. At about six, the beer truck came to bring the full drums and collect the empties; but already in the main room of the "Urbano Rattazzi" the sound of the polishers had begun, the machines that cleaned the floors for the day that was about to begin.

In moments of silence, in the heart of the night, next door, in Signorina Margariti's room, an intense talking would suddenly burst forth, mingled with little explosions of laughter, questions and answers, all in the same falsetto female voice; the deaf woman couldn't distinguish the act of thinking from the act of speaking aloud and at all hours of the day or even when she woke up late at night, whenever she became involved in a thought, a memory, a regret, she started talking to herself, distributing the dialogue among various speakers. Luckily her soliloquies, in their intensity, were incomprehensible; and yet they filled one with the uneasiness of sharing personal indiscretions.

During the day, when I went into the kitchen to ask her for some hot water to shave with (she couldn't hear a knock and I had to get within her eyeshot to make her aware of my presence), I would catch her talking to the mirror, smiling and grimacing, or seated, staring into the void, telling herself some story; then she would suddenly collect her wits and say: "Oh, I was talking to the cat," or else, "I'm sorry, I didn't see you; I was saying my prayers" (she was very devout). But most of the time she didn't realize she had been overheard.

To tell the truth she did talk to the cat often. She could make long speeches to him, for hours, and on certain evenings I heard her repeating "Pss . . . pss . . . kitty . . . here, kitty . . ." at the window, waiting for him to come back from his roaming along the balconies, roofs, and terraces. He was a scrawny, half-wild cat, with blackish fur that was gray every time he came home, as if he collected all the dust and soot of the neighborhood. He ran away from me if he even glimpsed me in the distance and would hide under the furniture, as if I had beaten him at the very least, though I never paid any attention to him. But when I was out, he surely visited my room: the freshly washed white shirt which the landlady set on the marble top of the dresser was always found with the cat's sooty paw prints on its collar and front. I would start shouting curses, which I quickly cut short because the deaf woman couldn't hear me, and so I then went into the other room to lay the disaster before her eyes. She was sorry, she hunted for the cat to punish him; she explained that no doubt when she had gone into my room to take the shirt, the cat had followed her without her noticing him; and she must have shut him up inside and the animal had jumped up on the dresser, to release his anger at being locked in.

I had only three shirts and I was constantly giving them to her to wash because—perhaps it was the still disordered life I led, with the office to be straightened out—after half a day my shirt was already dirty. I was often forced to go to the office with the cat's prints on my collar.

Sometimes I found his prints also on the pillowcase. He had probably remained shut inside after having followed Signorina Margariti when she came to "turn down the bed" in the evening.

It was hardly surprising that the cat was so dirty: you only had to put your hand on the railing of the landing to find your palm striped with black. Every time I came home, as I fumbled with the keys at four padlocks or keyholes, then stuck my fingers into the slats of the shutters to open and close the French window, I got my hands so dirty that when I came into the room I had to hold them in the air, to avoid leaving prints, while I went straight to the basin.

Once my hands were washed and dried I immediately felt better, as if I had regained the use of them, and I began touching and shifting those few objects around me. Signorina Margariti, I must say, kept the room fairly clean; as far as dusting went, she dusted every day; but there were times when, if I put my hand in certain places she couldn't reach (she was very short and had short arms, too), I drew it out all velvety with dust and I had to go back to the basin and wash immediately.

My books constituted my most serious problem: I had arranged them on the étagère, and they were the only things that gave me the impression this room was mine; the office left me plenty of free time and I would gladly have spent some hours in my room, reading. But books collect God knows how much dust: I would choose one from the shelf, but then before opening it, I had to rub it all over with a rag, even along the tops of the pages, and then I had to give it a good banging: a cloud of dust rose from it. Afterward I washed my hands again and finally flung myself down on the bed to read. But as I leafed through the book, it became hopeless, I could feel that film of dust on my fingertips, becoming thicker, softer all the time, and it spoiled my pleasure in reading. I got up, went back to the basin, rinsed my hands once more, but now I felt that my shirt was also dusty, and my suit. I would have resumed reading but now my hands were clean and I didn't like to dirty them again. So I decided to go out.

Naturally, all the operations of leaving: the shutters, the railing, the locks, reduced my hands to a worse state than ever, but I had to leave them as they were until I reached the office. At the office, the moment I arrived, I ran to the toilet to wash them; the office towel, however, was black with finger marks; as I began to dry my hands, I was already dirtying them again.

I SPENT my first working days at the Institute putting my desk in order. In fact, the desk assigned me was covered with correspondence, documents, files, old newspapers; until then it had obviously been a kind of clearinghouse where anything with no proper place of its own was put. My first impulse was to make a clean sweep; but then I saw there was material that could be useful for the magazine, and other things of some interest which I decided to examine at my leisure. In short, I finally removed nothing from the desk and actually added a lot of things, but not in disorder: on the contrary, I tried to keep everything tidy. Naturally, the papers that had been there before were very dusty and infected the new papers with their dirt. And since I set great store by my neatness, I had given orders to the cleaning woman not to touch anything, so each day a little more dust settled on the papers, especially on the writing materials, the stationery, the envelopes, and so on, which soon looked old and soiled and were irksome to touch.

And in the drawers it was the same story. There dusty papers from decades past were stratified, evidence of the desk's long career through various offices, public and private. No matter what I did at that desk, after a few minutes I felt impelled to go wash my hands.

My colleague Signor Avandero, on the contrary, kept his hands—delicate little hands, but with a certain nervous hardness—always clean, well groomed, the nails polished, uniformly clipped.

"Excuse me for asking, but," I tried saying to him, "don't you find, after you've been here a while, I mean . . . have you noticed how one's hands become dirty?"

"No doubt," Avandero answered, with his usual composed manner, "you have touched some object or paper that wasn't perfectly dusted. If you'll allow me to give you a word of advice, it's always a good idea to keep the top of one's desk completely clear."

In fact, Avandero's desk was clear, clean, shining, with only the file he was dealing with at that moment and the ballpoint pen he held in his hand. "It's a habit," he added, "that the President feels is very important." In fact, Commendatore Cordà had said the same thing to me: the executive who keeps his desk completely clear is a man who never lets matters pile up, who starts every problem on the road to its solution. But Cordà was never in the office, and when he was there he stayed a quarter of an hour, had great graphs and statistical charts brought in to him, gave rapid, vague orders to his subordinates, assigned the various duties to one or the other without bothering about the degree of difficulty of each assignment, rapidly dictated a few letters to the stenographer, signed the outgoing correspondence, and was off.

Not Avandero, though. Avandero stayed in the office morning and afternoon, he created an impression of working very hard and of giving the stenographers and the typists a lot to do, but he managed never to keep a sheet of paper on his desk more than ten minutes. I simply couldn't stomach this business; I began to keep an eye on him and I noticed that these papers, though they didn't stay long on his desk, were soon bogged down somewhere else. Once I caught him when, not knowing what to do with some letters he was holding, he had approached my desk (I had stepped out to wash my hands a moment) and was placing them there, hiding them under a file. Afterward he quickly took his handkerchief from his breast pocket, wiped his hands, and went back to his place, where the ballpoint pen lay parallel to an immaculate sheet of paper.

I could have gone in at once and put him in an awkward spot. But I was content with having seen him; it was enough for me to know how things worked.

SINCE I entered my room from the landing, the rest of Signorina Margariti's apartment remained unexplored territory to me. The Signorina lived alone, renting two rooms on the courtyard, mine and another next to it. I knew nothing of the other tenant except his heavy tread late at night and early in the morning (he was a police sergeant, I learned, and was never to be seen during the day). The rest of the apartment, which must have been rather vast, was all the landlady's.

Sometimes I was obliged to go look for her because she was wanted on the telephone; she couldn't hear it ring, so in the end I went and answered. Holding the receiver to her ear, however, she could hear fairly well; and long phone conversations with the other ladies of the parish sodality were her pastime. "Telephone! Signorina Margariti! You're wanted on the telephone!" I would shout, pointlessly, through the apartment, knocking, even more pointlessly, at the doors. As I made these rounds, I got to know a series of living rooms, parlors, pantries, all cluttered with old-fashioned, pretentious furniture, with floor lamps and bric-à-brac, pictures and statues and calendars; the rooms were all in order, polished, gleaming with wax, with snowy-white lace antimacassars on the armchairs, and without even a speck of dust.

At the end of one of these rooms I would finally discover Signorina Margariti, busy waxing the parquet floor or rubbing the furniture, wearing a faded wrapper and a kerchief around her head. I would point in the direction of the telephone, with violent gestures; the deaf woman would run and grasp the receiver, beginning another of her endless chats, in tones not unlike those of her conversations with the cat.

Going back to my room then, seeing the basin shelf or the lampshade with an inch of dust, I would be seized by a great anger: that woman spent the whole day keeping her rooms as shiny as a mirror and she wouldn't even wave a dustcloth over my place. I went back, determined to make a scene, with gestures and grimaces; and I found her in the kitchen, and this kitchen was kept even worse than my room: the oilcloth on the table all worn and stained, dirty cups on top of the cupboard, the floor tiles cracked and blackened. And I was speechless, because I knew the kitchen was the only place in the whole house where that woman really lived, and the rest, the richly adorned rooms constantly swept and waxed, were a kind of work of art on which she lavished her dreams of beauty; and to cultivate the perfection of those rooms she was self-condemned not to live in them, never to enter them as mistress of the house, but only as cleaning woman, spending the rest of her day amid grease and dust.

Purification came out every two weeks and carried, as a subtitle, "of the Air from Smoke, from Chemical Exhaust, and from the Products of Combustion." The magazine was the official organ of the IPUAIC, "The Institute for the Purification of the Urban Atmosphere in Industrial Centers." The IPUAIC was affiliated with similar associations in other countries, which sent us their bulletins and their pamphlets. Often international conventions were held, especially to discuss the serious problem of smog.

I had never concerned myself with questions of this sort, but I knew that putting out a magazine in a specialized field is not as hard as it seems. You follow the foreign reviews, you have certain articles translated, and with them and a subscription to a clipping agency you can quickly compile a news column; then there are those two or three technical contributors who never fail to send in a little article; also the Institute, no matter how inactive it is, always has some communication or agenda to be printed in bold type; and there is the advertiser who asks you to publish, as an article, the description of his latest patented device. Then when a convention is held, you can devote at least one whole issue to it, from beginning to end, and you will still have papers and reports left over to run in the following issues, whenever you have two or three columns you don't know how to fill.

The editorial as a rule was written by the President. But Commendatore Cordà, always extremely busy (he was Chairman of the Board of a number of industries, and he could only devote his odd free moments to the Institute), began asking me to draft it, incorporating the ideas that he described to me with vigor and clarity. I would then submit my draft to him on his return. He traveled a great deal, our President, because his factories were scattered more or less throughout the country; but of all his activities, the Presidency of the IPUAIC, a purely honorary position, was the one, he told me, which gave him the greatest satisfaction, "because," as he explained, "it's a battle for an ideal."

As far as I was concerned, I had no ideals, nor did I want to have any; I only wanted to write an article he would like, to keep my job, which was no better or worse than another, and to continue my life, no better or worse than any other possible life. I knew Cordà's opinions ("If everyone followed our example, atmospheric purity would already be . . .") and his favorite expressions ("We are not utopians, mind you, we are practical men who . . ."), and I would write the article just as he wished, word for word. What else could I write? What I thought with my own mind? That would produce a fine article, all right! A fine optimistic vision of a functional, productive world! But I had only to turn my mood inside out (which wasn't hard for me because it was like attacking myself) to summon the impetus necessary for an inspired editorial by our President.

"We are now on the threshold of a solution to the problem of volatile wastes," I wrote, "a solution which will be more quickly achieved"—and I could already see the President's satisfied look—"as the active inspiration given Technology by Private Initiative"—at this point Cordà would raise one hand, to underline my words—"is implemented by intelligent action on the part of the Government, always so prompt . . ."

I read this piece aloud to Signor Avandero. Resting his neat little hands on a white sheet of paper in the center of his desk, Avandero looked at me with his usual, inexpressive politeness.

"Well? Don't you like it?" I asked him.

"Oh, yes, yes indeed," he hastened to say.

"Listen to the ending: 'To answer the catastrophic predictions from some quarters concerning industrial civilization, we once more affirm that there will not be (nor has there ever been) any contradiction between an economy in free, natural expansion and the hygiene necessary to the human organism' "—from time to time I glanced at Avandero, but he didn't raise his eyes from that white sheet of paper—" 'between the smoke of our productive factories and the green of our incomparable natural beauty. . . .' Well, what do you say to that?"

Avandero stared at me for a moment with his dull eyes, his lips pursed. "I'll tell you: your article does express very well what might be called the substance of our Institute's final aim, yes, the goal toward which all its efforts are directed. . . ."

"Hmm . . ." I grumbled. I must confess that from a punctilious character like my colleague I expected a less tortuous approval.

I presented the article to Commendatore Cordà on his arrival a couple of days later. He read it with care, in my presence. He finished reading, put the pages in order, and seemed about to reread it from the beginning, but he only said: "Good." He thought for a moment, then repeated: "Good." Another pause, and then: "You're young." He warded off an objection I had no intention of making. "No, that's not a criticism, believe me. You are young, you have faith, you look far ahead. However, if I may say so, the situation is serious, yes, more serious than your article would lead the reader to believe. Let's speak frankly: the danger of air pollution in the big cities is huge, we have the analyses, the situation is grave. And precisely because it is grave, we are here to solve it. If we don't solve it, our cities, too, will be suffocated by smog."

He had risen and was pacing back and forth. "We aren't hiding the difficulties from ourselves. We aren't like the others, especially those who are in a position which should force them to think about this, and who instead don't give a damn. Or worse: try to block our efforts."

He stood squarely in front of me, lowered his voice: "Because you are young, perhaps you believe everybody agrees with us. But they don't. We are only a handful. Attacked from all sides, that's the truth of it. All sides. And yet we won't give up. We speak out. We act. We will solve the problem. This is what I would like to feel more strongly in your article, you understand?"

I understood perfectly. My insistent pretense of holding opinions contrary to my own had carried me away, but now I would be able to give the article just the right emphasis. I was to show it to the President again in three days' time. I rewrote from beginning to end. In the first two thirds of it I drew a grim picture of the cities of Europe devoured by smog, and in the final third I opposed this with the image of an exemplary city, our own, clean, rich in oxygen, where a rational complex of sources of production went hand in hand with . . . et cetera.

To concentrate better, I wrote the article at home, lying on my bed. A shaft of sunlight fell obliquely into the deep courtyard, entered through the panes, and I saw it cut across the air of my room with a myriad of impalpable particles. The counterpane must be impregnated with them; in a little while, I felt, I would be covered by a blackish layer, like the slats of the blind, like the railing of the balcony.

When I read the new draft to Signor Avandero, I had the impression he didn't dislike it. "This contrast between the situation in our cities and that in others," he said, "which you no doubt expressed according to our President's instructions, has really come off quite well."

"No, no, the President didn't mention that to me, it was

my own idea," I said, a bit annoyed despite myself because my colleague didn't believe me capable of any initiative.

Cordà's reaction, on the other hand, took me by surprise. He laid the typescript on the desk and shook his head. "We still don't understand each other," he said at once. He began to give me figures on the city's industrial production, the coal, the fuel oil consumed daily, the traffic of vehicles with combustion engines. Then he went on to meteorological data, and in every case he made a summary comparison with the larger cities of northern Europe. "We are a great, foggy industrial city, you realize; therefore smog exists here, too, we have no less smog than anywhere else. It is impossible to declare, as rival cities here in our own country try to do, that we have less smog than foreign cities. You can write this quite clearly in the article, you *must* write it! We are one of the cities where the problem of air pollution is most serious, but at the same time we are the city where most is being done to counteract the situation! At the same time, you understand?"

I understood, and I also understood that he and I would never understand each other. Those blackened façades of the houses, those dulled panes of glass, those window sills on which you couldn't lean, those human faces almost erased, that haze which now, as autumn advanced, lost its humid, bad-weather stink and became a kind of quality of all objects, as if each person and each thing had less shape every day, less meaning or value. Everything that was, for me, the substance of a general wretchedness, for men like him was surely the sign of wealth, supremacy, power, and also of danger, destruction, and tragedy, a way of feeling filled—suspended there—with a heroic grandeur.

I wrote the article a third time. It was all right, at last. Only the ending ("Thus we are face to face with a terrible

problem, affecting the destiny of society. Will we solve it?")
caused him to raise an objection.

"Isn't that a bit too uncertain?" he asked. "Won't it discourage our readers?"

The simplest thing was to remove the question mark and shift the pronoun. "We will solve it." Just like that, without any exclamation point: calm self-confidence.

"But doesn't that make it seem too easy? As if it were just a routine matter?"

We agreed to repeat the words. Once with the question mark and once without. "Will we solve it? We will solve it."

But didn't this seem to postpone the solution to a vague future time? We tried putting it in the present tense. "Are we solving it? We are solving it." But this didn't have the right ring.

Writing an article always proceeds in the same way. You begin by changing a comma, and then you have to change a word, then the word order of a sentence, and then it all collapses. We argued for half an hour. I suggested using different tenses for the question and the answer: "Will we solve it? We are solving it." The President was enthusiastic and from that day on his faith in my talents never wavered.

ONE NIGHT the telephone woke me, the special, insistent ring of a long-distance call. I turned on the light: it was almost three o'clock. Even before making up my mind to get out of bed, rush into the hall, and grope for the receiver in the dark, even before that, at the first jolt in my sleep, I already knew it was Claudia.

Her voice now gushed from the receiver and it seemed to

come from another planet; with my eyes barely open I had a sensation of sparks, dazzle, which were instead the shifting tones of her unceasing voice, that dramatic excitement she always put into everything she said, and which now arrived even here, at the end of the squalid hall in Signorina Margariti's apartment. I realized I had never doubted Claudia would find me; on the contrary, I had been expecting nothing else for all this time.

She didn't bother to ask what I had been doing in the meanwhile, or how I had ended up there, nor did she explain how she had traced me. She had heaps of things to tell me, extremely detailed things, and yet somehow vague, as her talk always was, things that took place in environments unknown and unknowable to me.

"I need you, quickly, right away. Take the first train. . . ."

"Well, I have a job here. . . . The Institute . . ."

"Ah, perhaps you've run into Senator . . . Tell him . . ."

"No, no, I'm just the . . ."

"Darling, you will leave right away, won't you?"

How could I tell her I was speaking from a place full of dust, where the blinds' slats were covered with a gritty black grime, and there were cat's prints on my collar, and this was the only possible world for me, while hers, her world, could exist for me, or seem to exist, only through an optical illusion? She wouldn't even have listened, she was too accustomed to seeing everything from above and the wretched circumstances that formed the texture of my life naturally escaped her. What was her whole relationship with me if not the outcome of this superior distraction of hers, thanks to which she had never managed to realize I was a modest provincial newspaperman without a future, without ambitions?

And she went on treating me as if I were part of high society, the world of aristocrats, magnates, and famous artists, where she had always moved and where, in one of those chance encounters that occur at the beach, I had been introduced to her one summer. She didn't want to admit it, because that would mean admitting she had made a mistake; so she went on attributing talents to me, authority, tastes I was far from possessing; but my real, fundamental identity was a mere detail, and in mere details she did not want to be contradicted.

Now her voice was becoming tender, affectionate: this was the moment that—without even confessing it to myself —I had been waiting for, because it was only in moments of amorous abandon that everything separating us disappeared and we discovered we were just two people, and it didn't matter who we were. We had barely embarked on an exchange of amorous words when, behind me, a light came on beyond a glass door, and I could hear a grim cough. It was the door of my fellow tenant, the police sergeant, right there, beside the telephone. I promptly lowered my voice. I resumed the interrupted sentence, but now that I knew I was overheard, a natural reserve made me tone down my loving expressions, until they were reduced to a murmuring of neutral phrases, almost unintelligible. The light in the next room went off, but from the other end of the wire protests began: "What did you say? Speak louder! Is that all you have to tell me?"

"But I'm not alone. . . ."

"What? Who's with you?"

"No, listen, you'll wake up the tenants, it's late. . . ."

By now she was in a fury, she didn't want explanations, she wanted a reaction from me, a sign of warmth on my side, something that would burn up the distance between us. But my answers had become cautious, whining, soothing. "No, Claudia, you see, I . . . don't say that, I swear, I beg you, Claudia, I . . ." In the sergeant's room the light came on again. My love talk became a mumble, my lips pressed to the receiver.

In the courtyard the kitchen workers were rolling the empty beer drums. Signorina Margariti, in the darkness of her room, began chatting, punctuating her words with brief bursts of laughter, as if she had visitors. The fellow tenant uttered a Southern curse. I was barefoot, standing on the tiles of the hall, and from the other end of the wire Claudia's passionate voice held out her hands to me, and I was trying to run toward her with my stammering, but each time we were about to cast a bridge between us, it crumbled to bits a moment later, and the impact of reality crushed and denied all our words of love, one by one.

AFTER THAT first time, the telephone took to ringing at the oddest hours of the day and night, and Claudia's voice, tawny and speckled, leaped into the narrow hall, with the heedless spring of a leopard who doesn't know he is throwing himself into a trap, and since he doesn't know, he manages, with a second leap, as he came, to find the path out again: and he hasn't realized anything. And I, torn between suffering and love, joy and cruelty, saw her mingling with this scene of ugliness and desolation, with the loud-speaker of the "Urbano Rattazzi" which blurted out: "Noodle soup," with the dirty bowls in Signorina Margariti's sink, and I felt that by now even Claudia's image must be stained by it all. But no, it ran off, along the wire, intact, aware of nothing, and each time I was left alone with the void of her absence.

Sometimes Claudia was gay, carefree, she laughed, said senseless things to tease me, and in the end I shared in her gaiety, but then the courtyard, the dust saddened me all the more because I had been tempted to believe life could be different. At other times, instead, Claudia was gripped by a feverish anxiety and this anxiety then was added to the appearance of the place where I lived, to my work as managing editor of *Purification,* and I couldn't rid myself of it, I lived in the expectation of another, more dramatic call which would waken me in the heart of the night, and when I finally did hear her voice again, surprisingly different, gay or languid, as if she couldn't even remember the torment of the night before, rather than liberated, I felt bewildered, lost.

"What did you say? You're calling from Taormina?"

"Yes, I'm down here with some friends, it's lovely, come right away, catch the next plane!"

Claudia always called from different cities, and each time, whether she was in a state of anxiety or of exuberance, she insisted that I join her at once, to share that mood with her. Each time I started to give her a careful explanation of why it was absolutely impossible for me to travel, but I couldn't continue because Claudia, not listening to me, had already shifted to another subject, usually a harangue against me, or else an unpredictable hymn of praise, for some casual expression of mine which she found abominable or adorable.

When the allotted time of the call was up and the day or night operator said: "Three minutes. Do you wish to continue?" Claudia would shout: "When are you arriving, then?" as if it were all agreed. I would stammer some answer, and we ended by postponing final arrangements to another call she would make to me or I was to make to her. I knew that in the meanwhile Claudia would change all her plans and the urgency of my trip would come up again, surely, but in different circumstances which would then justify further postponements; and yet a kind of remorse lingered in me, because the impossibility of my joining her was not so absolute, I could ask for an advance on my next month's salary and a leave of three or four days with some pretext; these hesitations gnawed at me.

Signorina Margariti heard nothing. If, crossing the hall, she saw me at the telephone, she greeted me with a nod, unaware of the storms raging within me. But not the fellow tenant. From his room he heard everything and he was obliged to apply his policeman's intuition every time the phone's ring made me jump. Luckily, he was hardly ever in the house, and therefore some of my telephone conversations even managed to be self-confident, nonchalant, and, depending on Claudia's humor, we could create an atmosphere of amorous exchange where every word took on a warmth, an intimacy, an inner meaning. On other occasions, however, she was in the best of moods and I was instead blocked, I answered only in monosyllables, with reticent, evasive phrases: the sergeant was behind his door, a few feet from me; once he opened it a crack, stuck out his dark, mustachioed face, and examined me. He was a little man, I must say, who in other circumstances wouldn't have made the least impression on me; but there, late at night, seeing each other face to face for the first time, in that lodginghouse for poor wretches, I making and receiving amorous long-distance calls of half an hour, he just coming off duty, both of us in our pajamas, we undeniably hated each other.

Often Claudia's conversation included famous names, the people she saw regularly. First of all, I don't know anybody; secondly, I can't bear attracting attention; so if I absolutely had to answer her, I tried not to mention any names, I used paraphrases, and she couldn't understand why and it made her angry. Politics, too, is something I've always steered clear of, precisely because I don't like making myself conspicuous; and now, besides, I was working for a government-sponsored Institute and I had made it a rule to know nothing of either party; and Claudia—God knows what got into her one evening—asked me about certain Members of Parliament. I had to give her some kind of answer, then and there, with the sergeant behind the door. "The first one . . . the first name you mentioned, of course . . ."

"Who? Whom do you mean?"

"That one, yes, the big one, no, smaller . . ."

In other words, I loved her. And I was unhappy. But how could she have understood this unhappiness of mine? There are those who condemn themselves to the most gray, mediocre life because they have suffered some grief, some misfortune; but there are also those who do the same thing because their good fortune is greater than they feel they can sustain.

I TOOK my meals in certain fixed-price restaurants, which, in this city, are all run by Tuscan families, all of them related among themselves, and the waitresses are all girls from a town called Altopascio, and they spend their youth here, but with the thought of Altopascio constantly in their minds, and they don't mingle with the rest of the city; in the evening they go out with boys from Altopascio, who work here in the kitchens of the restaurants or perhaps in factories, but still sticking close to the restaurants as if they were outlying districts of their village; and these girls and these boys marry and some go back to Altopascio, others stay here to work in their relatives' or their fellow townsmen's restaurants, saving up until one day they can open a restaurant of their own.

The people who eat in those restaurants are what you would expect: apart from travelers, who change all the time, the habitual customers are unmarried white-collar workers, even some spinster typists, and a few students or soldiers. After a while these customers get to know one another and they chat from table to table, and at a certain point they eat at the same table, groups of people who at first didn't know one another and then ended up by falling into the habit of always eating together.

They all joked, too, with the Tuscan waitresses, good-natured jokes, obviously; they asked about the girls' boyfriends, they exchanged witticisms, and when there was nothing else to talk about they started on television, saying who was nice and who wasn't among the faces they had seen in the latest programs.

But not me, I never said anything except my order, which for that matter was always the same: spaghetti with butter, boiled beef, and greens, because I was on a diet; and I never called the girls by name even though by then I too had learned their names, but I preferred to go on saying "Signorina" so as not to create an impression of familiarity: I had happened upon that restaurant by chance, I was just a random customer, perhaps I would continue going there every day for God knows how long, but I wanted to feel as if I were passing through, here today and somewhere else tomorrow, otherwise the place would get on my nerves.

Not that they weren't likable. On the contrary: both the staff and the clientele were good, pleasant people, and I enjoyed that cordial atmosphere around me; in fact, if it hadn't existed, I would probably have felt something was lacking, but still I preferred to look on, without taking part in it. I avoided conversing with the other customers, not even greeting them, because, as everyone knows, it's easy enough to strike up an acquaintance, but then you're involved; somebody says: "What's on this evening?" and you end up all together watching television or going to the movies, and after that evening you're caught up in a group of people who mean nothing to you, and you have to tell them your business, and listen to theirs.

I tried to sit down at a table by myself, I would open the morning or evening paper (I bought it on my way to the office and took a glance at the headlines then, but I waited to read it until I was at the restaurant), and then I read through it from beginning to end. The paper was of great use to me when I couldn't find a seat by myself and had to sit down at a table where there was already someone else; I plunged into my reading and nobody said a word to me. But I always tried to find a free table and for this reason I was careful to put off as late as possible the hour of my meals, so I turned up there when most of the customers had already left.

There was the disadvantage of the crumbs. Often I had to sit down at a table where another customer had just got up and left the table covered with crumbs; so I avoided looking down until the waitress came to clear away the dirty dishes and glasses, sweeping up all the remains into the cloth and changing it. At times this task was done hastily and between the top cloth and the bottom one there were bread crumbs, and they distressed me.

The best thing, at lunchtime for example, was to discover the hour when the waitresses, thinking that by then no more customers would be coming, clean up everything properly and prepare the tables for the evening; then the whole family, owners, waitresses, cooks, dishwashers, set one big table and finally sit down to eat, themselves. At that moment I would go in, saying: "Oh, perhaps I'm too late. Can you give me something to eat?"

"Why, of course! Sit down wherever you like! Lisa, serve the gentleman."

I sat down at one of those lovely clean tables, a cook went back into the kitchen, I read the paper, I ate calmly, I listened to the others laughing at their table, joking and telling stories of Altopascio. Between one dish and the next I would have to wait perhaps a quarter of an hour, because the waitresses were sitting there eating and chatting, and I would finally make up my mind to say: "An orange, please, Signorina. . . ." And they would say: "Yes sir! Anna, you go. Oh, Lisa!" But I liked it that way, I was happy.

I finished eating, finished reading the paper, and went out with the paper rolled up in my hand, I went home, I climbed up to my room, threw the paper on the bed, washed my hands. Signorina Margariti kept watch to see when I came in and when I left, because the moment I was outside she came into my room to take the newspaper. She didn't dare ask me for it, so she took it away in secret and secretly she put it back on the bed before I came home again. She seemed to be ashamed of this, as if of a somehow frivolous curiosity; in fact she read only one thing, the obituaries.

Once when I came in and found her with the paper in her

hand, she was deeply embarrassed and felt obliged to explain: "I borrow it every now and then to see who's dead, you know, forgive me, but, sometimes, you know, I have acquaintances among the dead. . . ."

THANKS TO this idea of postponing mealtimes, for example by going to the movies on certain evenings, I came out of the film late, my head a bit giddy, to find a dense darkness shrouding the neon signs, an autumnal mist, which drained the city of dimensions. I looked at the time, I told myself there probably was nothing left to eat in those little restaurants, or in any case I was off my usual schedule and I wouldn't be able to get back to it again, so I decided to have a quick bite standing at the counter in the "Urbano Rattazzi" beer hall, just below where I lived.

Entering the place from the street was not just a passage from darkness to light: the very consistency of the world changed. Outside, all was shapeless, uncertain, dispersed, and here it was full of solid forms, of volumes with a thickness, a weight, brightly colored surfaces, the red of the ham they were slicing at the counter, the green of the waiters' Tyrolean jackets, the gold of the beer. The place was full of people and I, who in the streets was accustomed to look on passers-by as faceless shadows and to consider myself another faceless shadow among so many, rediscovered here all of a sudden a forest of male and female faces, as brightly colored as fruit, each different from the rest and all unknown. For a moment I hoped still to retain my own ghostly invisibility in their midst, then I realized that I, too, had become like them, a form so precise that even the mirrors reflected it, with the stubble of beard that had grown since morning, and there was no possible refuge; even the smoke which drifted in a thick cloud to the ceiling from all the lighted cigarettes in the place was a thing apart with its out-line and its thickness and didn't modify the substance of the other things.

I made my way to the counter, which was always very crowded, turning my back on the room full of laughter and words from each table, and as soon as a stool became free I sat down on it, trying to attract the waiter's attention, so he would set before me the square cardboard coaster, a mug of beer, and the menu. I had trouble making them notice me, here at the "Urbano Rattazzi" over which I kept vigil night after night, whose every hour, every jolt I knew, and the noise in which my voice was lost was the same I heard rise every evening up along the rusty iron railings.

"Gnocchi with butter, please," I said, and finally the waiter behind the counter heard me and went to the micro-phone to declare: "One gnocchi with butter!" and I thought of how that cadenced shout emerged from the loud-speaker in the kitchen, and I felt as if I were simultaneously here at the counter and up there, lying on my bed in my room, and I tried to break up in my mind and muffle the words that constantly crisscrossed among the groups of jolly people eat-ing and drinking and the clink of glasses and cutlery until I could recognize the noise of all my evenings.

Transparently, through the lines and colors of this part of the world, I was beginning to discern the features of its re-verse, of which I felt I was the only inhabitant. But perhaps the true reverse was here, brightly lighted and full of open eyes, whereas the side that counted in every way was the shadowy part, and the "Urbano Rattazzi" beer hall existed only so you could hear that distorted voice in the darkness, "One gnocchi with butter!" and the clank of the metal drums, and so the street's mist might be pierced by the sign's halo, by the square of misted panes against which vague human forms were outlined.

ONE MORNING I was wakened by a call from Claudia, but this wasn't long distance; she was in the city, at the station, she had just that moment arrived and was calling me because, in getting out of the sleeping car, she had lost one of the many cases that comprised her luggage.

I got there barely in time to see her coming out of the station, at the head of a procession of porters. Her smile had none of that agitation she had transmitted to me by her phone call a few minutes before. She was very beautiful and elegant; each time I saw her I was amazed to see I had forgotten what she was like. Now she suddenly pronounced herself enthusiastic about this city and she approved my idea of coming to live here. The sky was leaden; Claudia praised the light, the streets' colors.

She took a suite in a grand hotel. For me to go into the lobby, address the desk clerk, have myself announced by phone, follow the bellboy to the elevator, caused endless uneasiness and dismay. I was deeply moved that Claudia, because of certain business matters of hers but in reality perhaps to see me, had come to spend a few days here: moved and embarrassed, as the abyss between her way of life and mine yawned before me.

And yet, I managed to get along fairly well during that busy morning and even to turn up briefly at the office to draw an advance on my next pay-check, foreseeing the exceptional days that lay ahead of me. There was the problem of where to take her to eat: I had little experience of de luxe restaurants or special regional places. As a start, I had the idea of taking her up to one of the surrounding hills.

I hired a taxi. I realized now that, in that city, where nobody earning above a certain figure was without a car (even my colleague Avandero had one), I had none, and anyway I wouldn't have known how to drive one. It had never mattered to me in the least, but in Claudia's presence I was ashamed. Claudia, on the other hand, found everything quite natural, because—she said—a car in my hands would surely spell disaster; to my great annoyance she loudly made light of my practical ability and based her admiration of me on other talents, though there was no telling what they were.

So we took a taxi; we hit on a rickety car, driven by an old man. I tried to make a joke of how flotsam, wreckage, inevitably comes to life around me, but Claudia wasn't upset by the ugliness of the taxi, as if these things couldn't touch her, and I didn't know whether to be relieved or to feel more than ever abandoned to my fate.

We climbed up to the green backdrop of hills that girdles the city to the east. The day had cleared into a gilded autumnal light, and the colors of the countryside, too, were turning gold. I embraced Claudia, in that taxi; if I let myself give way to the love she felt for me, perhaps that green and gold life would also yield to me, the life that, in blurred images (to embrace her, I had removed my eyeglasses), ran by at either side of the road.

Before going to the little restaurant, I told the elderly driver to take us somewhere to look at the view, up higher. We got out of the car. Claudia, with a huge black hat, spun around, making the folds of her skirt swell out. I darted here and there, pointing out to her the whitish crest of the Alps that emerged from the sky (I mentioned the names of the mountains at random, since I couldn't recognize them) and, on this side, the broken and intermittent outline of the hill with villages and roads and rivers, and down below, the city like a network of tiny scales, opaque or glistening, meticulously aligned. A sense of vastness had seized me; I don't know whether it was Claudia's hat and skirt, or the view. The air, though this was autumn, was fairly clear and unpolluted, but it was streaked by the most diverse kinds of condensation: thick mists at the base of the mountains, wisps of fog over the rivers, chains of clouds, stirred variously by the wind. We were there leaning over the low wall: I, with my arm around her waist, looking at the countless aspects of the landscape, suddenly gripped by a need to analyze, already dissatisfied with myself because I didn't command sufficiently the nomenclature of the places and the natural phenomena; she ready instead to translate sensations into sudden gusts of love, into effusions, remarks that had nothing to do with any of this. At this point I saw the thing. I grabbed Claudia by the wrist, clasping it hard. "Look! Look down there!"

"What is it?"

"Down there! Look! It's moving!"

"But what is it? What do you see?"

How could I tell her? There were other clouds or mists which, according to how the humidity condenses in the cold layers of air, are gray or bluish or whitish or even black, and they weren't so different from this one, except for its uncertain color, I couldn't say whether more brownish or bituminous; but the difference was rather in a shadow of this color which seemed to become more intense first at the edges, then in the center. It was, in short, a shadow of dirt, soiling everything and changing—and in this too it was different from the other clouds—its very consistency, because it was heavy, not clearly dispelled from the earth, from the speck-

led expanse of the city over which it flowed slowly, gradually erasing it on one side and revealing it on the other, but
trailing a wake, like slightly dirty strands, which had no end.

"It's smog!" I shouted at Claudia. "You see that? It's a
cloud of smog!"

But she wasn't listening to me, she was attracted by something she had seen flying, a flight of birds; and I stayed
there, looking for the first time, from outside, at the cloud
that surrounded me every hour, at the cloud I inhabited and
that inhabited me, and I knew that, in all the variegated
world around me, this was the only thing that mattered to
me.

THAT EVENING I took Claudia to supper at the "Urbano
Rattazzi" beer hall, because except for my cheap restaurants
I knew no other place and I was afraid of ending up somewhere too expensive. Entering the "Urbano Rattazzi" with a
girl like Claudia was a new experience: the waiters in their
Tyrolean jackets all sprang to attention, they gave us a good
table, they rolled over the trolleys with the specialties. I tried
to act the nonchalant escort but at the same time I felt I had
been recognized as the tenant of the furnished room over
the courtyard, the customer who had quick meals on a stool
at the counter. This state of mind made me clumsy, my conversation was dull, and soon Claudia became angry with
me. We fell into an intense quarrel; our voices were
drowned by the noise of the beer hall, but we had trained on
us not only the eyes of the waiters, prompt to obey Claudia's
slightest sign, but also those of the other customers, their
curiosity aroused by this beautiful, elegant, imposing
woman in the company of such a meek-looking man. And I

realized that the words of our argument were followed by everyone, also because Claudia, in her unconcern for the people around her, made no effort to disguise her feelings. I felt they were all waiting only for the moment when Claudia, infuriated, would get up and leave me there alone, making me once more the anonymous man I had always been, the man nobody notices any more than one would notice a spot of damp on the wall.

Instead, as always, the quarrel was followed by a tender, amorous understanding; we had reached the end of the meal and Claudia, knowing I lived nearby, said: "I'll come up to your place."

Now I had taken her to the "Urbano Rattazzi" because it was the only restaurant I knew of that sort, not because it was near my room; in fact, I was on pins and needles at the very thought that she might form some idea of the house where I lived just by glancing at the doorway of the building, and I had relied chiefly on her flightiness.

Instead, she wanted to go up there. Telling her about the room, I exaggerated its squalor, to turn the whole event into something grotesque. But as she went up and crossed the landing, she noticed only the good aspects: the ancient and rather noble architecture of the building, the functional way in which those old apartments were laid out. We went in, and she said: "Why, what are you talking about? The room is wonderful. What more do you want?"

I turned at once to the basin, before helping her off with her coat, because as usual I had soiled my hands. But not she, she moved around, her hands fluttering like feathers among the dusty furnishings.

The room was soon invaded by those alien objects: her hat with its little veil, her fox stole, velvet dress, organdy slip, satin shoes, silk stockings; I tried to hang everything up in the wardrobe, put things in the drawers, because I thought that if they stayed out they would soon be covered with traces of soot.

Now Claudia's white body was lying on the bed, on that bed from which, if I hit it, a cloud of dust would rise, and she reached out with one hand to the shelf next to it and took a book. "Be careful, it's dusty!" But she had already opened it and was leafing through it, then she dropped it to the floor. I was looking at her breasts, still those of a young girl, the pink, pointed tips, and I was seized with torment at the thought that some dust from the book's pages might have fallen on them, and I extended my hand to touch them lightly in a gesture resembling a caress but intended, really, to remove from them the bit of dust I thought had settled there.

Instead, her skin was smooth, cool, undefiled; and as I saw in the lamp's cone of light a little shower of dust specks floating in the air, soon to be deposited also on Claudia, I threw myself upon her in an embrace which was chiefly a way of covering her, of taking all the dust upon myself so that she would be safe from it.

AFTER SHE had left (a bit disappointed and bored with my company, despite her unshakable determination to cast on others a light that was all her own), I flung myself into my editorial work with redoubled energy, partly because Claudia's visit had made me miss many hours in the office and I was behind with the preparation of the next number, and also because the subject the biweekly *Purification* dealt with no longer seemed so alien to me as it had at the beginning.

The editorial was still unwritten, but this time Commendatore Cordà had left me no instructions. "You handle it. Be careful, however." I began to write one of the usual diatribes, but gradually, as one word led to the next, I found myself describing how I had seen the cloud of smog rubbing over the city, how life went on inside that cloud, and the façades of the old houses, all jutting surfaces and hollows where a black deposit thickened, and the façades of the modern houses, smooth, monochrome, squared off, on which little by little dark, vague shadows grew, as on the office workers' white collars, which never stayed clean more than half a day. And I wrote that, true, there were still people who lived outside the cloud of smog, and perhaps there always would be, people who could pass through the cloud and stop right in its midst and then come out, without the tiniest puff of smoke or bit of soot touching their bodies, disturbing their different pace, their otherworldly beauty, but what mattered was everything that was inside that smog, not what lay outside it: only by immersing oneself in the heart of the cloud, breathing the foggy air of these mornings (winter was already erasing the streets in a formless mist), could one reach the bottom of the truth and perhaps be free of it. My words were all an arguement with Claudia; I realized this at once and tore up the article without even having Avandero read it.

Signor Avandero was somebody I hadn't yet fathomed. One Monday morning I came into the office, and what did I find? Avandero with a sun tan! Yes, instead of his usual face the color of boiled fish, his skin was something between red and brown, with a few marks of burning on his forehead and his cheeks.

"What's happened to you?" I asked (calling him *tu,* as we had been addressing each other recently).

"I've been skiing. The first snowfall. Perfect, nice and dry. Why don't you come too, next Sunday?"

From that day on, Avandero made me his confidant, sharing with me his passion for skiing. Confidant, I say, because in discussing it with me, he was expressing something more than a passion for a technical skill, a geometrical precision of movements, a functional equipment, a landscape reduced to a pure white page; he, the impeccable and obsequious employee, put into his words a secret protest against his work, a polemical attitude he revealed in little chuckles, as if of superiority, and in little malicious hints: "Ah, yes, that's *purification,* all right! I leave the smog to the rest of you. . . ." Then he promptly corrected himself, saying: "I'm joking, of course. . . ." But I had realized that he, apparently so loyal, was another one who didn't believe in the Institute or the ideas of Commendatore Cordà.

One Saturday afternoon I ran into him, Avandero, all decked out for skiing, with a vizored cap like a blackbird's beak, heading for a large bus already assailed by a crowd of men and women skiers. He greeted me, with his smug little manner: "Are you staying in the city?"

"Yes, I am. What's the use of going away? Tomorrow night you'll already be back in the soup again."

He frowned, beneath his blackbird's vizor. "What's the city for, then, except to get out of on Saturday and Sunday?" And he hurried to the bus, because he wanted to suggest a new way of arranging the skis on the top.

For Avandero, as for hundreds and thousands of other people who slaved all week at gray jobs just to be able to run off on Sunday, the city was a lost world, a mill grinding out the means to escape it for those few hours and then return from country excursions, from trout fishing, and then from the sea, and from the mountains in summer, from the

115

snapshots. The story of his life—which, as I saw him regularly, I began to reconstruct year by year—was the story of his means of transportation: first a motorbike, then a scooter, then a proper motorcycle, now his cheap car, and the years of the future were already designated by visions of cars more and more spacious, faster and faster.

THE NEW number of *Purification* should already have gone to press, but Commendatore Cordà hadn't yet seen the proofs. I was expecting him that day at the IPUAIC, but he didn't show up, and it was almost evening when he telephoned for me to come to him at his office at the Wafd, to bring him the proofs there because he couldn't get away. In fact, he would send his car and driver to pick me up.

The Wafd was a factory of which Cordà was managing director. The huge automobile, with me huddled in one corner, my hands and the folder of proofs on my knees, carried me through unfamiliar outskirts, drove along a blind wall, entered, saluted by watchmen, through a broad gateway, and deposited me at the foot of the stairway to the directors' offices.

Commendatore Cordà was at his desk, surrounded by a group of executives, examining certain accounts or production plans spread out on enormous sheets of paper, which spilled over the sides of the desk. "Just one minute, please," he said to me, "I'll be right with you."

I looked beyond his shoulder: the wall behind him was a single pane of glass, a very wide window that dominated the whole expanse of the plant. In the foggy evening only a few shadows emerged; in the foreground there was the outline of a chain hoist which carried up huge buckets of—I believe—

iron tailings. You could see the row of metal receptacles rise in a series of jerks, with a slight swaying that seemed to alter a bit the outline of the pile of mineral, and I thought I saw a thick cloud rise from it into the air and settle on the glass of the Commendatore's office.

At that moment he gave orders for the lights to be turned on; suddenly against the outside darkness the glass seemed covered by a tiny frosting, surely composed of iron particles, glistening like the stardust of a galaxy. The pattern of shadows outside was broken up; the lines of the smokestacks in the distance became more distinct, each crowned by a red puff, and over these flames, in contrast, the black, inky streak was accentuated as it invaded the whole sky and you could see incandescent specks rise and whirl within it.

Cordà was now examining with me the *Purification* proofs and, immediately entering the different field of enthusiasms, receiving the mental stimulation of his position as President of the IPUAIC, he discussed the articles in our bulletin with me and with the Wafd executives. And though I had so often, in the offices of the Institute, given free rein to my natural dependent's antagonism, mentally declaring myself on the side of the smog, the smog's secret agent who had infiltrated the enemy's headquarters, I now realized how senseless my game was, because Cordà himself was the smog's master; it was he who blew it out constantly over the city, and the IPUAIC was a creature of the smog, born of the need to give those working to produce the smog some hope of a life that was not all smog, and yet, at the same time, to celebrate its power.

Cordà, pleased with the issue, insisted on taking me home in the car. It was a night of thick fog. The driver proceeded slowly, because beyond the faint headlights you couldn't see a thing. The President, carried away by one of his bursts of general optimism, was outlining the plans of the city of the future, with garden districts, factories surrounded by flower beds and pools of clear water, installations of rockets that would sweep the sky clear of the smoke from the stacks. And he pointed into the void outside, beyond the windows, as if the things he was imagining were already there; I listened to him, perhaps frightened or perhaps in admiration, I couldn't say, discovering how the clever captain of industry coexisted in him with the visionary, and how each needed the other.

At a certain point I thought I recognized my neighborhood. "Stop here, please. This is where I get out," I said to the driver. I thanked Cordà, said good night, and got out of the car. When it had driven off, I realized I had been mistaken. I was in an unfamiliar district, and I could see nothing of my surroundings.

AT THE restaurant I went on having my meals alone, sheltered behind my newspaper. And I noticed that there was another customer who behaved as I did. Sometimes, when no other places were free, we ended up at the same table, facing each other with our unfolded papers. We read different ones: mine was the newspaper everybody read, the most important in the city; surely I had no reason to attract attention, to look different from the others, by reading a different paper, or to seem (if I had read the paper of the stranger at my table) a man with strong political ideas. I had always given political opinions and parties a wide berth, but there, at the restaurant table, on certain evenings, when I put the newspaper down, my fellow diner said: "May I?" motioning to it, and offering me his own: "If you'd like to have a look at this one . . ."

And so I glanced at his paper, which was, you might say, the reverse of mine, not only because it supported opposing ideas, but because it dealt with things that didn't even exist for the other paper: workers who had been discharged, mechanics whose hands had been caught in their machinery (it also published the photographs of these men), charts with the figures of welfare payments, and so on. But above all, the more my paper tried to be witty in the writing of its articles and to attract the reader with amusing minor events, for example the divorce cases of pretty girls, the more this other paper used expressions that were always the same, repetitious, drab, with headlines that emphasized the negative side of things. Even the printing of the paper was drab, cramped, monotonous. And I found myself thinking: "Why, I like it!"

I tried to explain this impression to my casual companion, naturally taking care not to comment on individual news items or opinions (he had already begun by asking me what I thought of a certain report from Asia) and trying at the same time to play down the negative aspect of my view, because he seemed to me the sort of man who doesn't accept criticisms of his position and I had no intention of launching an argument.

Instead, he seemed to be following his own train of thought, where my opinion of his paper must have been superfluous or out of place. "You know," he said, "this paper still isn't the way it should be? It isn't the paper I'd like it to be."

He was a short but well-proportioned young man, dark, with carefully combed curly hair, his face still a boy's, pale, pink-cheeked, with regular, refined features, long black lashes, a reserved, almost haughty manner. He dressed with rather fastidious care. "There's still too much vagueness, a lack of precision," he went on, "especially in what concerns *our* affairs. The paper still resembles the others too much. The kind of paper I mean should be mostly written by its readers. It should try to give scientifically exact information about everything that goes on in the world of production."

"You're a technical expert in some factory, are you?" I asked.

"Skilled worker."

We introduced ourselves. His name was Omar Basaluzzi. When he learned that I worked for the IPUAIC, he became very much interested and asked me for some data to use in a report he was preparing. I suggested some publications to him (things in the public domain, as a matter of fact; I wasn't giving away any office secrets, as I remarked to him, just in case, with a little smile). He took out a notebook and methodically wrote down the information, as if he were compiling a bibliography.

"I'm interested in statistical studies," he said, "a field where our organization is far behind." We put on our over-coats, ready to leave. Basaluzzi had a rather sporty coat, elegantly cut, and a little cap of rainproof canvas. "We're very far behind," he went on, "whereas, the way I look at it, it's a fundamental field. . . ."

"Does your work leave you time for these studies?" I asked him.

"I'll tell you," he said (he always answered with some hauteur, in a slightly smug, ex-cathedra manner), "it's all a question of method. I work eight hours a day in the factory, and then there's hardly an evening when I don't have some meeting to go to, even on Sunday. But you have to know how to organize your work. I've formed some study groups, among the young people in our plant. . . ."

"Are there many . . . like yourself?"

"Very few. Fewer all the time. One by one, they're getting rid of us. One fine day you'll see here"—and he pointed to the newspaper—"my own picture, with the headline: 'Another worker discharged in reprisal.' "

We were walking in the cold of the night; I was huddled in my coat, the collar turned up; Omar Basaluzzi proceeded calmly, talking, his head erect, a little cloud of steam emerging from his finely drawn lips, and every now and then he took his hand from his pocket to underline a point in his talk, and then he stopped, as if he couldn't go ahead until that point had been clearly established.

I was no longer following what he said; I was thinking that a man like Omar Basaluzzi didn't try to evade all the smoky gray around us, but to transform it into a moral value, an inner criterion.

"The smog . . ." I said.

"Smog? Yes, I know Cordà wants to play the modern industrialist. . . . Purify the atmosphere. . . . Go tell that to his workers! He surely won't be the one to purify it. . . . It's a question of social structure. . . . If we manage to change that, we will also solve the smog problem. We, not they."

He invited me to go with him to a meeting of union representatives from the different plants of the city. I sat at the back of a smoky room. Omar Basaluzzi took a seat at the table on the dais with some other men, all older than he. The room wasn't heated; we kept our hats and coats on.

One by one, the men who were to speak stood up and took their place beside the table; all of them addressed the public in the same way: anonymous, unadorned, with formulas for beginning their speech and for linking the arguments which must have been part of some rule because they all used them. From certain murmurs in the audience I realized a polemical statement had been made, but these were veiled polemics, which always began by approving what had been said before. Many of those who spoke seemed to have it in for Omar Basaluzzi; the young man, seated a bit sideways at the table, had taken a tooled-leather tobacco pouch from his pocket and a stubby English pipe which he filled with slow movements of his small hands. He smoked in cautious puffs, his eyes slightly closed, one elbow on the table, his cheek resting in his hand.

The hall had filled with smoke. One man suggested opening a little, high window for a moment. A cold gust changed the air but soon the fog began coming in from outside, and you could hardly see the opposite end of the room. From my seat I examined that crowd of backs, motionless in the cold, some with upturned collars, and the row of bundled-up forms at the table, with one man on his feet talking, as bulky as a bear, all surrounded, impregnated now by that fog, even their words, their stubbornness.

CLAUDIA CAME back in February. We went to have lunch in an expensive restaurant on the river, at the end of the park. Beyond the windows we looked at the shore and the trees that, with the color of the air, composed a picture of ancient elegance.

We couldn't understand each other. We argued on the subject of beauty. "People have lost the sense of beauty," Claudia said.

"Beauty has to be constantly invented," I said.

"Beauty is always beauty; it's eternal."

"Beauty is born always from some conflict."

"What about the Greeks?"

"Well, what about them?"

"Beauty is civilization!"

"And so . . ."

"Therefore . . ."

We could have gone on like this all day and all night.

"This park, this river . . ."

("This park, this river," I thought, "can only be marginal, a consolation to us for the rest; ancient beauty is powerless against new ugliness.")

"This eel . . ."

In the center of the restaurant there was a glass tank, an aquarium, and some huge eels were swimming inside it.

"Look!"

Some customers were approaching, important people, a family of well-to-do gourmets: mother, father, grown daughter, adolescent son. With them was the *maître d'hôtel,* an enormous, corpulent man in frock coat, stiff white shirt; he was grasping the handle of a little net, the kind children use for catching butterflies. The family, serious, intent, looked at the eels; at a certain point the mother raised her hand and pointed out an eel. The *maître d'hôtel* dipped the net into the aquarium, with a rapid swoop he caught the animal and drew it out of the water. The eel writhed and struggled in the net. The *maître d'hôtel* went off toward the kitchen, holding the net with the gasping eel straight out in front of him like a lance. The family watched him go off, then they sat down at the table, to wait until the eel came back, cooked.

"Cruelty . . ."

"Civilization . . ."

"Everything is cruel . . ."

Instead of having them call a taxi, we left on foot. The lawns, the tree trunks, were swathed in that veil which rose from the river, dense, damp, here still a natural phenomenon. Claudia walked protected by her fur coat, its wide collar, her muff, her fur hat. We were the two shadowy lovers who form a part of the picture.

"Beauty . . ."

"Your beauty . . ."

"What good is it? As far as that goes . . ."

I said: "Beauty is eternal."

"Ah, now you're saying what I said before, eh?"

"No, the opposite."

"It's impossible to discuss anything with you," she said.

She moved off as if she wanted to go on by herself, along the path. A layer of fog was flowing just over the earth: the fur-covered silhouette proceeded as if it weren't touching the ground.

I SAW Claudia back to her hotel that evening, and we found the lobby full of gentlemen in dinner jackets and ladies in long, low-cut dresses. It was carnival time, and a charity ball was being held in the hotel ballroom.

"How marvelous! Will you take me? I'll just run and put on an evening dress!"

I'm not the sort who goes to balls and I felt ill at ease.

"But we don't have an invitation . . . and I'm wearing a brown suit. . . ."

"I never need an invitation . . . and you're my escort."

She ran up to change. I didn't know where to turn. The

place was full of girls wearing their first evening dress, pow-
dering their faces before going into the ballroom, exchang-
ing excited whispers. I stood in a corner, trying to imagine I
was a shop clerk who had come there to deliver a package.

The elevator door opened. Claudia stepped out, in a
sweeping skirt, pearls on a pink bodice, a little diamond-
studded mask. I couldn't play the role of clerk any more. I
went over to her.

We went in. All eyes were on her. I found a mask to put
on, a kind of clown's face with a long nose. We started danc-
ing. When Claudia twirled around, the other couples
stepped back to watch her; as I'm a very bad dancer, I
wanted to stay in the midst of the crowd, so there was a kind
of hide-and-seek. Claudia complained that I wasn't the least
bit jolly, that I didn't know how to enjoy myself.

At the end of one dance, as we were going back to our
table, we passed a group of ladies and gentlemen, standing
on the dance floor. "Oh!" There I was, face to face with
Commendatore Cordà. He was in full dress, with a little
orange paper hat on his head. I had to stop and say hello to
him. "Why, it *is* you, then! I thought so, but I wasn't sure,"
he said, but he was looking at Claudia, and I realized he
meant he would never have expected to see me with a
woman like her, I looking the same as usual, in the suit I
wore to the office.

I had to make the introductions; Cordà kissed Claudia's
hand, introduced her to the other older men who were with
him, and Claudia, absent as always and superior, paid no
attention to the names (as I was saying to myself: "My
God! Is that who he is?" because they were all big shots in
industry). Then Cordà introduced me: "And this is the
managing editor of our periodical, you know, *Purification,*

the paper I put out. . . ." I realized they were all a bit intimidated by Claudia, and they were talking nonsense. So then I felt less timid myself.

I also realized something else was about to happen, namely that Cordà could hardly wait to ask Claudia to dance. I said: "Well then, we'll see you later. . . ." I waved expansive good-bys and led Claudia back to the dance floor, as she said: "Wait a minute, you don't know how to dance to this, can't you hear the music?"

All I could hear or feel was that, in some way not yet clear even to those men, I had spoiled their evening when I appeared at Claudia's side, and this was the only satisfaction I could derive from the ball. *"Cha cha cha . . ."* I sang softly, pretending to dance with steps I didn't know how to make, holding Claudia only lightly by the hand so that she could move on her own.

It was carnival time; why shouldn't I have some fun? The little toy trumpets blared, fluttering their long fringes, handfuls of confetti pattered like crumbling mortar on the backs of the tailcoats and on the bare shoulders of the women, it slipped inside the low-cut gowns and the men's collars; and from chandelier to floor, where they collected in limp piles pushed about by the shuffling of the dancers, streamers unrolled like strips of bare fibers or like wires left hanging among collapsed walls in a general destruction.

"YOU CAN accept the ugly world the way it is, because you know you have to destroy it," I said to Omar Basaluzzi. I spoke partly to provoke him, otherwise it was no fun.

"Just a moment," Omar said, setting down the little cup of coffee he had been raising to his lips. "We never say: It has to get worse before it can get better. We want to improve things. . . . No reformism, and no extremism. We . . ."

I was following my train of thought; he, his. Ever since that time in the park with Claudia, I had been looking for a new image of the world which would give a meaning to our grayness, which would compensate for all the beauty that we were losing, or would save it. . . . "A new face for the world."

The worker unzipped a black leather briefcase and took out an illustrated weekly. "You see?" There was a series of photographs. An Asiatic race, with fur caps and boots, blissfully going to fish in a river. In another photograph there was that same race, going to school; a teacher was pointing out, on a sheet, the letters of an incomprehensible alphabet. Another illustration showed a feast day and they all wore dragon heads, and in the middle, among the dragons, a tractor was advancing with a man's portrait over it. At the end there were two men, still in fur caps, operating a power lathe.

"You see? This is it," he said, "the other face of the world."

I looked at Basaluzzi. "You people don't wear fur caps, you don't fish for sturgeon, you don't play with dragons."

"What of it?"

"So your group doesn't resemble those people in any way, except for this . . ." and I pointed to the lathe, "which you already have."

"No, no, it'll be the same here as there, because it's man's conscience that will change, for us as it has for them, we'll be new inside ourselves, even before we are new outside . . ." Basaluzzi said, and he went on leafing through the magazine. On another page there were photographs of

127

blast furnaces and of workers with goggles over their eyes and fierce expressions. "Oh, there'll be problems then, too, you mustn't think that overnight . . ." he said. "For quite a while it'll be hard: production . . . But a big step forward will have been made. . . . Certain things won't happen, as they do now . . ." and he started speaking of the same things he always talked about, the problems that concerned him, day in and day out.

I realized that, for him, whether or not that new dawn ever came mattered less than one might think, because what counted for him was the line of his life, which was not to change.

"There'll always be trouble, of course. . . . It won't be an earthly paradise. . . . We're not saints, after all. . . ."

Would the saints change their lives, if they knew heaven didn't exist?

"They fired me last week," Omar Basaluzzi said.

"And now what?"

"I'm doing union work. Maybe next autumn one of the bosses will retire."

He was on his way to the Wafd, where there had been a violent demonstration that morning. "Want to come with me?"

"Eh! That's the one place I mustn't be seen. You understand why."

"I mustn't be seen there either. I'd get the comrades in trouble. We'll watch from a café nearby."

I went with him. Through the windows of a little café we saw the workers coming off their shift walk through the gates, wheeling their bicycles, or crowding toward the streetcars, their faces already prepared for sleep. Some of them, obviously forewarned, came into the café and went at once to Omar; and so a little group was formed, which went off to one side to talk.

I understood nothing of their grievances and I was trying to discover what was different between the faces of the countless men who swarmed through the gates surely thinking of nothing but their family and Sunday, and these others who had stopped with Omar, the stubborn ones, the tough ones. And I could find no mark that distinguished them: the same aged or prematurely old faces, product of the same life: the difference was inside.

And then I studied the faces and the words of the latter group, to see if I could distinguish the ones whose actions were based on the thought "The day will come . . ." and those for whom, as for Omar, whether the day really came or not didn't matter. And I saw they couldn't be distinguished, because perhaps they all belonged to the second category, even those few whose impatience or ready speech might make them seem to be in the first category.

And then I didn't know what to look at so I looked at the sky. It was an early spring day and over the houses of the outskirts the sky was luminous, blue, clear; however, if I looked at it carefully, I could see a kind of shadow, a smudge, as if on an old, yellowed snapshot, like the marks you see through a spectroscope. Not even the fine season would cleanse the sky.

Omar Basaluzzi had put on a pair of dark glasses with thick frames and he continued talking in the midst of those men, precise, expert, proud, a bit nasal.

IN *Purification* I published a news item I had found in a foreign paper concerning pollution of the air by atomic radiation. It was in small type and Commendatore Cordà didn't notice it in the galleys, but he read it when the paper was printed and he then sent for me.

"My God, I have to keep an eye on every little thing; I ought to have a hundred eyes, not two!" he said. "What came over you? What made you publish that piece? This isn't the sort of thing our Institute should bother with. Not by a long shot! And then, without a word to me! On such a delicate question! Now they'll say we've started printing propaganda!"

I answered with a few words of defense: "Well, sir, since it was a question of air pollution . . . I'm sorry, I thought . . ."

I had already taken my leave when Cordà called me back. "See here, do you really believe in this danger of radioactivity? I mean, do you really think it's so serious?"

I remembered certain data from a scientific congress, and I repeated the information to him. Cordà listened to me, nodding, but irked.

"Hmph, what awful times we have to live in, my friend!" he blurted out at one point, and he was again the Cordà I knew so well. "It's the risk we have to run. There's no turning back the clock, because big things are at stake, my boy, big things!"

He bowed his head for a few moments. "We, in our field," he went on, "not wanting to overestimate the role we play, of course, still . . . we make our contribution, we're equal to the situation."

"That's certain, sir. I'm absolutely convinced of that." We looked at each other, a bit embarrassed, a bit hypocritical. The cloud of smog now seemed to have grown smaller, a tiny little puff, a cirrus, compared to the looming atomic mushroom.

I left Commendatore Cordà after a few more vague, affirmative words, and once again it wasn't clear whether his real battle was fought for or against the cloud.

After that, I avoided any mention of atomic explosions or radioactivity in the headlines, but in each number I tried to slip some information on the subject into the columns devoted to technical news, and even into certain articles; in the midst of the data on the percentages of coal or fuel oil in the urban atmosphere and their physiological consequences, I added analogous data and examples drawn from zones affected by atomic fallout. Neither Cordà nor anyone else mentioned these to me again, but this silence, rather than please me, confirmed my suspicion that absolutely nobody read *Purification*.

I had a file where I kept all the material concerning nuclear radiation, because as I read through the papers with an eye trained to select usable news items and articles, I always found something on that subject and I saved it. A clipping service, too, to which the Institute had subscribed, sent us more and more clippings about atomic bombs, while those about smog grew fewer all the time.

So every day my eye fell upon statistics of terrible diseases, stories about fishermen overtaken in the middle of the ocean by lethal clouds, guinea pigs born with two heads after some experiments with uranium. I raised my eyes to the window. It was late June, but summer hadn't yet begun: the weather was oppressive, the days were smothered in a gloomy haze, during the afternoon hours the city was immersed in a light like the end of the world, and the passersby seemed shadows photographed on the ground after the body had flown away.

The normal order of the seasons seemed changed, intense cyclones coursed over Europe, the beginning of summer was marked by days heavily charged with electricity, then by weeks of rain, by sudden heat waves and sudden resurgences of March-like cold. The papers denied that these atmospheric disorders could be in any way connected with the effects of the bombs; only a few solitary scientists seemed to sustain this notion (and, for that matter, it was hard to discover if they were trustworthy) and, with them, the anonymous voice of the man in the street, always ready, of course, to give credence to the most disparate ideas.

Even I became irritated when I heard Signorina Margariti talking foolishly about the atomic bomb, warning me to take my umbrella to the office that morning. But to be sure, when I opened the blinds, at the livid sight of the courtyard, which in that false luminosity seemed a network of stripes and spots, I was tempted to draw back, as if a discharge of invisible particles were being released from the sky at that very moment.

This burden of unsaid things transformed them into superstition, influenced the banal talk about the weather, once considered the most harmless subject of conversation. Now people avoided mentioning the weather, or if they had to say it was raining or it had cleared they were filled with a kind of shame, as if some obscure responsibility of ours were being kept quiet. Signor Avandero, who lived through the weekdays in preparation for his Sunday excursion, had assumed a false indifference toward the weather; it seemed totally hypocritical to me, and servile.

I put out a number of *Purification* in which there wasn't one article that didn't speak of radioactivity. Even this time I had no trouble. It wasn't true, however, that nobody read the paper; people read it, all right, but by now they had become inured to such things, and even if you wrote that the

132

end of the human race was at hand nobody paid any attention.

The big weeklies also published reports that should have made you shudder, but people now seemed to believe only in the colored photographs of smiling girls on the cover. One of these weeklies came out with a photograph of Claudia on its cover; she was wearing a bathing suit, and was making a turn on water skis. With four thumbtacks, I pinned it on the wall of my furnished room.

EVERY MORNING and every afternoon I continued to go to that neighborhood of quiet avenues where my office was located, and sometimes I recalled the autumn day when I had gone there for the first time, when in everything I saw I had looked for a sign, and nothing had seemed sufficiently gray and squalid to suit the way I felt. Even now my gaze looked only for signs; I had never been able to see anything else. Signs of what? Signs that referred one to the other, into infinity.

At times I happened to encounter a mule-drawn cart: a two-wheeled cart going down an avenue, laden with sacks. Or else I found it waiting outside the door of a building, the mule between the shafts, his head low, and on top of the pile of sacks, a little girl.

Then I realized there wasn't only one of these carts going around that section; there were several of them. I couldn't say just when I began to notice this; you see so many things without paying attention to them; maybe these things you see have an effect on you but you aren't aware of it; and then you begin to connect one thing with the other and suddenly it all takes on meaning. The sight of those carts, without my consciously thinking of them, had a soothing effect on me, because an unusual encounter, as with a rustic cart in the midst of a city that is all automobiles, is enough to remind you that the world is never all one thing.

And so I began to pay attention to them: a little girl with pigtails sat on top of the white mountain of sacks reading a comic book, then a heavy man came from the door of the building with a couple of sacks and put those, too, on the cart, turned the handle of the brake and said "Gee" to the mule, and they went off, the little girl still up there, still reading. And then they stopped at another doorway; the man unloaded some sacks from the cart and carried them inside.

Farther ahead, in the opposite lane of the avenue, there was another cart, with an old man at the reins, and a woman who went up and down the front steps of the buildings with huge bundles on her head.

I began to notice that on the days when I saw the carts I was happier, more confident, and those days were always Mondays: so I learned that Monday is the day when the laundrymen go through the city with their carts, bringing back the clean laundry and taking away the dirty.

Now that I knew about it, the sight of the laundry carts no longer escaped me: all I had to do was see one as I went to work in the morning, and I would say to myself: "Why, of course, it's Monday!" and immediately afterward another would appear, following a different route, with a dog barking after it, and then another going off in the distance so I could see only its load from behind, the sacks with yellow and white stripes.

Coming home from the office I took the streetcar,

through other streets, noisier and more crowded, but even there the traffic had to stop at a crossing as the long-spoked wheels of a laundry cart rolled by. I glanced into a side street, and by the sidewalk I saw the mule with bundles of laundry that a man in a straw hat was unloading.

That day I took a much longer route than usual to come home, still encountering the laundrymen. I realized that for the city this was a kind of feast day, because everyone was happy to give away the clothes soiled by the smoke and to wear again the whiteness of fresh linen, even if only for a short while.

The following Monday I decided to follow the laundry carts to see where they went afterward, once they had made their deliveries and picked up their work. I walked for a while at random, because I first followed one cart, then another, until at a certain point I realized that they were all finally going in the same direction, there were certain streets where they all passed eventually, and when they met or lined up one after the other they hailed one another with calm greetings and jokes. And so I went on following them, losing them, over a long stretch, until I was tired, but before leaving them I had learned that there was a village of laundries: the men were all from an outlying town called Barca Bertulla.

One day, in the afternoon, I went there. I crossed a bridge over a river, and was virtually in the country, the highways were flanked still by a row of houses, but immediately behind them all was green. You couldn't see the laundries. Shady pergolas surrounded the wineshops, along the canals interrupted by locks. I went on, casting my gaze beyond each farmyard gate and along each path. Little by little I left the built-up area behind, and now rows of poplars grew along the road, marking the banks of the frequent canals. And there in the background, beyond the poplars, I saw a meadow of white sails: laundry hung out to dry.

I turned into a path. Broad meadows were crisscrossed with lines, at eye level, and on these lines, piece after piece, was hung the laundry of the whole city, the linen still wet and shapeless, every item the same, with wrinkles the cloth made in the sun, and in each meadow this whiteness of long lines of washing was repeated. (Other meadows were bare, but they too were crossed by parallel lines, like vineyards without vines.)

I wandered through the fields white with hanging laundry, and I suddenly wheeled about at a burst of laughter. On the shore of a canal, above one of the locks, there was the ledge of a pool, and over it, high above me, their sleeves rolled up, in dresses of every color, were the red faces of the washerwomen, who laughed and chattered; the young ones' breasts bobbing up and down inside their blouses, and the old, fat women with kerchiefs on their heads; and they moved their round arms back and forth in the suds and they wrung out the twisted sheets with an angular movement of the elbows. In their midst the men in straw hats were unloading baskets in separate piles, or were also working with the square coarse soap, or else beating the wet cloth with wooden paddles.

By now I had seen, and I had nothing to say, no reason to pry. I turned back. At the edge of the highway a little grass was growing and I was careful to walk there, so as not to get my shoes dusty and to keep clear of the passing trucks. Between the fields, the hedgerows, and the poplars, I continued to follow with my eyes the washing pools, the signs on certain low buildings: STEAM LAUNDRY, LAUNDRY CO-OPERATIVE OF BARCA BERTULLA, the fields where the women passed with baskets as if harvesting grapes, and picked the dry linen from the lines, and the countryside in the sun gave forth its greenness amid that white, and the water flowed away swollen with bluish bubbles. It wasn't much, but for me, seeking only images to retain in my eyes, perhaps it was enough.

The Argentine Ant

Translated by Archibald Colquhoun

WHEN WE came to settle here we did not know about the ants. We'd be all right here, it seemed that day; the sky and green looked bright, too bright, perhaps, for the worries we had, my wife and I—how could we have guessed about the ants? Thinking it over, though, Uncle Augusto may have hinted at this once: "You should see the ants over there . . . they're not like the ones here, those ants . . ." but that was just said while talking of something else, a remark of no importance, thrown in perhaps because as we talked we happened to notice some ants. Ants, did I say? No, just one single lost ant, one of those fat ants we have at home (they seem fat to me, now, the ants from my part of the country). Anyway, Uncle Augusto's hint did not seem to detract from the description he gave us of a region where, for some reason which he was unable to explain, life was easier and jobs were not too difficult to find, judging by all those who had set themselves up there—though not, apparently, Uncle Augusto himself.

On our first evening here, noticing the twilight still in the air after supper, realizing how pleasant it was to stroll along those lanes toward the country and sit on the low walls of a bridge, we began to understand why Uncle Augusto liked it. We understood it even more when we found a little inn which he used to frequent, with a garden behind, and squat, elderly characters like himself, though rather more blustering and noisy, who said they had been his friends; they too were men without a trade, I think, workers by the hour, though one said he was a clockmaker, but that may have been bragging; and we found they remembered Uncle Augusto by a nickname, which they all repeated among general guffaws; we noticed, too, rather stifled laughter from a woman in a knitted white sweater who was fat and no longer young, standing behind the bar.

And my wife and I understood what all this must have meant to Uncle Augusto; to have a nickname and spend light evenings joking on the bridges and watch for that knitted sweater to come from the kitchen and go out into the orchard, then spend an hour or two next day unloading sacks for the spaghetti factory; yes, we realized why he always regretted this place when he was back home.

I would have been able to appreciate all this too, if I'd been a youth and had no worries, or been well settled with the family. But as we were, with the baby only just recovered from his illness, and work still to find, we could do no more than notice the things that had made Uncle Augusto call himself happy; and just noticing them was perhaps rather sad, for it made us feel the difference between our own wretched state and the contented world around. Little things, often of no importance, worried us lest they should suddenly make matters worse (before we knew anything about the ants); the endless instructions given us by the owner, Signora Mauro, while showing us over the rooms, increased this feeling we had of entering troubled waters. I remember a long talk she gave us about the gas meter, and how carefully we listened to what she said.

"Yes, Signora Mauro. . . . We'll be very careful, Signora Mauro. . . . Let's hope not, Signora Mauro. . . ."

So that we did not take any notice when (though we remember it clearly now) she gave a quick glance all over the wall as if reading something there, then passed the tip of her finger over it, and brushed it afterward as if she had touched something wet, sandy, or dusty. She did not mention the word "ants," though, I'm certain of that; perhaps she considered it natural for ants to be there in the walls and roof; but my wife and I think now that she was trying to hide them from us as long as possible and that all her chatter and instructions were just a smoke screen to make other things seem important, and so direct our attention away from the ants.

When Signora Mauro had gone, I carried the mattresses inside. My wife wasn't able to move the cupboard by herself and called me to help. Then she wanted to begin cleaning out the little kitchen at once and got down on her knees to start, but I said: "What's the point, at this hour? We'll see to that tomorrow; let's just arrange things as best we can for tonight." The baby was whimpering and very sleepy, and the first thing to do was get his basket ready and put him to bed. At home we use a long basket for babies, and had brought one with us here; we emptied out the linen with which we'd filled it, and found a good place on the window ledge, where it wasn't damp or too far off the ground should it fall.

Our son soon went to sleep, and my wife and I began looking over our new home (one room divided in two by a partition—four walls and a roof), which was already showing signs of our occupation. "Yes, yes, whitewash it, of course we must whitewash it," I replied to my wife, glancing at the ceiling and at the same time taking her outside by an elbow. She wanted to have another good look at the toilet, which was in a little shack to the left, but I wanted to take a turn over the surrounding plot; for our house stood on a piece of land consisting of two large flower, or rather rough seed beds, with a path down the middle covered with an iron trellis, now bare and made perhaps for some dried-up climbing plant of gourds or vines. Signora Mauro had said she would let me have this plot to cultivate as a kitchen garden, without asking any rent, as it had been abandoned for so long; she had not mentioned this to us today, however, and we had not said anything as there were already too many other irons in the fire.

My intention now, by this first evening's walk of ours around the plot, was to acquire a sense of familiarity with the place, even of ownership in a way; for the first time in our lives the idea of continuity seemed possible, of walking evening after evening among beds of seeds as our circumstances gradually improved. Of course I didn't speak of those things to my wife; but I was anxious to see whether she felt them too; and that stroll of ours did, in fact, seem to have the effect on her which I had hoped. We began talking quietly, between long pauses, and we linked arms—a gesture symbolic of happier times.

Strolling along like this we came to the end of the plot, and over the hedge saw our neighbor, Signor Reginaudo, busy spraying around the outside of his house with a pair of bellows. I had met Signor Reginaudo a few months earlier when I had come to discuss my tenancy with Signora Mauro. I went up to greet him and introduce him to my wife. "Good evening, Signor Reginaudo," I said. "D'you re-member me?"

"Of course I do," he said. "Good evening! So you are our new neighbor now?" He was a short man with spectacles, in pajamas and a straw hat.

"Yes, neighbors, and among neighbors . . ." My wife began próducing a few vague pleasant phrases, to be polite: it was a long time since I'd heard her talk like that; I didn't particularly like it, but it was better than hearing her complain.

"Claudia," called our neighbor, "come here. Here are the new tenants of the Casa Laureri!" I had never heard our new home called that (Laureri, I learned later, was a previous owner), and the name made it sound strange. Signora Reginaudo, a big woman, now came out, drying her hands on her apron; they were an easygoing couple and very friendly.

"And what are you doing there with those bellows, Signor Reginaudo?" I asked him.

"Oh . . . the ants . . . these ants . . ." he said, and laughed as if not wanting to make it sound important.

"Ants?" repeated my wife in the polite detached tone she used with strangers to give the impression she was paying attention to what they were saying; a tone she never used with me, not even, as far as I can remember, when we first met.

We then took a ceremonious leave of our neighbors. But we did not seem to be enjoying really fully the fact of having neighbors, and such affable and friendly ones with whom we could chat so pleasantly.

On getting home we decided to go to bed at once. "D'you hear?" said my wife. I listened and could still hear the squeak of Signor Reginaudo's bellows. My wife went to the washbasin for a glass of water. "Bring me one too," I called, and took off my shirt.

"Oh!" she screamed. "Come here!" She had seen ants on the faucet and a stream of them coming up the wall.

We put on the light, a single bulb for the two rooms. The stream of ants on the wall was very thick; they were coming from the top of the door, and might originate anywhere. Our hands were now covered with them, and we held them out open in front of our eyes, trying to see exactly what they were like, these ants, moving our wrists all the time to prevent them from crawling up our arms. They were tiny wisps of ants, in ceaseless movement, as if urged along by the same little itch they gave us. It was only then that a name came to my mind: "Argentine ants," or rather, "the Argentine ant," that's what they called them; and now I came to think of it I must have heard someone saying that this was the country of "the Argentine ant." It was only now that I connected the name with a sensation, this irritating tickle spreading in every direction, which one couldn't get rid of by clenching one's fists or rubbing one's hands together as there always seemed to be some stray ant running up one's arm, or on one's clothes. When the ants were crushed, they became little black dots that fell like sand, leaving a strong acid smell on one's fingers.

"It's the Argentine ant, you know . . ." I said to my wife. "It comes from South America. . . ." Unconsciously my voice had taken on the inflection I used when wanting to teach her something; as soon as I'd realized this I was sorry, for I knew that she could not bear that tone in my voice and always reacted sharply, perhaps sensing that I was never very sure of myself when using it.

But instead she scarcely seemed to have heard me; she

was frenziedly trying to destroy or disperse that stream of ants on the wall, but all she managed to do was get numbers of them on herself and scatter others around. Then she put her hand under the faucet and tried to squirt water at them, but the ants went on walking over the wet surface; she couldn't even get them off by washing her hands.

"There, we've got ants in the house!" she repeated. "They were here before, too, and we didn't see them!"—as if things would have been very different if we had seen them before.

I said to her: "Oh, come, just a few ants! Let's go to bed now and think about it tomorrow!" And it occurred to me also to add: "There, just a few Argentine ants!" because by calling them by the exact name I wanted to suggest that their presence was already expected, and in a certain sense normal.

But the expansive feeling by which my wife had let herself be carried away during that stroll around the garden had now completely vanished; she had become distrustful of everything again and made her usual face. Nor was going to bed in our new home what I had hoped; we hadn't the pleasure now of feeling we were starting a new life, only a sense of dragging on into a future full of new troubles.

"All for a couple of ants," was what I was thinking— what I thought I was thinking, rather, for everything seemed different now for me too.

Exhaustion finally overcame our agitation, and we dozed off. But in the middle of the night the baby cried; at first we lay there in bed, always hoping it might stop and go to sleep again; this, however, never happened and we began asking ourselves: "What can be the matter? What's wrong with him?" Since he was better he had stopped crying at night.

"He's covered with ants!" cried my wife, who had gone

and taken him in her arms. I got out of bed too. We turned the whole basket upside down and undressed the baby completely. To get enough light for picking the ants off, half blind as we were from sleep, we had to stand under the bulb in the draft coming from the door. My wife was saying: "Now he'll catch cold." It was pitiable looking for ants on that skin which reddened as soon as it was rubbed. There was a stream of ants going along the windowsill. We searched all the sheets until we could not find another ant and then said: "Where shall we put him to sleep now?" In our bed we were so squeezed up against each other we would have crushed him. I inspected the chest of drawers and, as the ants had not got into that, pulled it away from the wall, opened a drawer, and prepared a bed for the baby there. When we put him in he had already gone to sleep. If we had only thrown ourselves on the bed we would have soon dozed off again, but my wife wanted to look at our provisions.

"Come here, come here! God! Full of 'em! Everything's black! Help!" What was to be done? I took her by the shoulders. "Come along, we'll think about that tomorrow, we can't even see now, tomorrow we'll arrange everything, we'll put it all in a safe place, now come back to bed!"

"But the food. It'll be ruined!"

"It can go to the devil! What can we do now? Tomorrow we'll destroy the ants' nest. Don't worry."

But we could no longer find peace in bed, with the thought of those insects everywhere, in the food, in all our things; perhaps by now they had crawled up the legs of the chest of drawers and reached the baby. . . . We got off to sleep as the cocks were crowing, but before long we had again started moving about and scratching ourselves and feeling we had ants in the bed; perhaps they had climbed up there, or stayed on us after all our handling of them. And so even the early morning hours were no refreshment, and we were very soon up, nagged by the thought of the things we had to do, and of the nuisance, too, of having to start an immediate battle against the persistent imperceptible enemy which had taken over our home.

The first thing my wife did was see to the baby: examine him for any bites (luckily, there did not seem to be any), dress and feed him—all this while moving around in the ant-infested house. I knew the effort of self-control she was making not to let out a scream every time she saw, for example, ants going around the rims of the cups left in the sink, and the baby's bib, and the fruit. She did scream, though, when she uncovered the milk: "It's black!" On top there was a veil of drowned or swimming ants. "It's all on the surface," I said. "One can skim them off with a spoon." But even so we did not enjoy the milk; it seemed to taste of ants.

I followed the stream of ants on the walls to see where they came from. My wife was combing and dressing herself, with occasional little cries of hastily suppressed anger. "We can't arrange the furniture till we've got rid of the ants," she said.

"Keep calm. I'll see that everything is all right. I'm just going to Signor Reginaudo, who has that powder, and ask him for a little of it. We'll put the powder at the mouth of the ants' nest. I've already seen where it is, and we'll soon be rid of them. But let's wait till a little later as we may be disturbing the Reginaudos at this hour."

My wife calmed down a little, but I didn't. I had said I'd seen the entrance to the ants' nest to console her, but the more I looked, the more new ways I discovered by which the ants came and went. Our new home, although it looked so smooth and solid on the surface, was in fact porous and honeycombed with cracks and holes.

I consoled myself by standing on the threshold and gazing at the plants with the sun pouring down on them; even the brushwood covering the ground cheered me, as it made me long to get to work on it: to clean everything up thoroughly, then hoe and sow and transplant. "Come," I said to my son. "You're getting moldy here." I took him in my arms and went out into the "garden." Just for the pleasure of starting the habit of calling it that, I said to my wife: "I'm taking the baby into the garden for a moment," then corrected myself: "Into our garden," as that seemed even more possessive and familiar.

The baby was happy in the sunshine and I told him: "This is a carob tree, this is a persimmon," and lifted him up onto the branches. "Now Papa will teach you to climb." He burst out crying. "What's the matter? Are you frightened?" But I saw the ants; the sticky tree was covered with them. I pulled the baby down at once. "Oh, lots of dear little ants . . ." I said to him, but meanwhile, deep in thought, I was following the line of ants down the trunk, and saw that the silent and almost invisible swarm continued along the ground in every direction between the weeds. How, I was beginning to wonder, shall we ever be able to get the ants out of the house when over this piece of ground, which had seemed so small yesterday but now appeared enormous in relation to the ants, the insects formed an uninterrupted veil, issuing from what must be thousands of underground nests and feeding on the thick sticky soil and the low vegetation? Wherever I looked I'd see nothing at first glance and would be giving a sigh of relief when I'd look closer and discover an ant approaching and find it formed part of a long procession, and was meeting others, often carrying crumbs and tiny bits of material much larger than themselves. In certain places, where they had perhaps collected some plant juice or animal remains, there was a guarding crust of ants stuck together like the black scab of a wound.

I returned to my wife with the baby at my neck, almost at a run, feeling the ants climbing up from my feet. And she said: "Look, you've made the baby cry. What's the matter?"

"Nothing, nothing," I said hurriedly. "He saw a couple of ants on a tree and is still affected by last night, and thinks he's itching."

"Oh, to have this to put up with too!" my wife cried. She was following a line of ants on the wall and trying to kill them by pressing the ends of her fingers on each one. I could still see the millions of ants surrounding us on that plot of ground, which now seemed immeasurable to me, and found myself shouting at her angrily: "What're you doing? Are you mad? You won't get anywhere that way."

She burst out in a flash of rage too. "But Uncle Augusto! Uncle Augusto never said a word to us! What a couple of fools we were! To pay any attention to that old liar!" In fact, what could Uncle Augusto have told us? The word "ants" for us then could never have even suggested the horror of our present situation. If he had mentioned ants, as perhaps he had—I won't exclude the possibility—we would have imagined ourselves up against a concrete enemy that could be numbered, weighed, crushed. Actually, now I think about the ants in our own parts, I remember them as reasonable little creatures, which could be touched and moved like cats or rabbits. Here we were face to face with an enemy like fog or sand, against which force was useless.

Our neighbor, Signor Reginaudo, was in his kitchen pouring liquid through a funnel. I called him from outside, and reached the kitchen window panting hard.

"Ah, our neighbor!" exclaimed Reginaudo. "Come in, come in. Forgive this mess! Claudia, a chair for our neighbor."

I said to him quickly: "I've come . . . please forgive the intrusion, but you know, I saw that you had some of that powder . . . all last night, the ants . . ."

"Oh, oh . . . the ants!" Signora Reginaudo burst out laughing as she came in, and her husband echoed her with a slight delay, it seemed to me, though his guffaws were noisier when they came. "Ha, ha, ha! . . . You have ants, too! Ha, ha, ha!"

Without wanting to, I found myself giving a modest smile, as if realizing how ridiculous my situation was, but now I could do nothing about it; this was in point of fact true, as I'd had to come and ask for help.

"Ants! You don't say so, my dear neighbor!" exclaimed Signor Reginaudo, raising his hands.

"You don't say so, dear neighbor, you don't say so!" exclaimed his wife, pressing her hands to her breast but still laughing with her husband.

"But you have a remedy, haven't you?" I asked, and the quiver in my voice could, perhaps, have been taken for a longing to laugh, and not for the despair I could feel coming over me.

"A remedy, ha, ha, ha!" The Reginaudos laughed louder than ever. "Have we a remedy? We've twenty remedies! A hundred . . . each, ha, ha, ha, each better than the other!"

They led me into another room lined with dozens of cartons and tins with brilliant-colored labels.

"D'you want some Profosfan? Or Mirminec? Or perhaps

Tiobroflit? Or Arsopan in powder or liquid form?" And still roaring with laughter he passed his hand over sprinklers with pistons, brushes, sprays, raising clouds of yellow dust, tiny beads of moisture, and a smell that was a mixture of a pharmacy and an agricultural depot.

"Have you really something that does the job?" I asked.

They stopped laughing. "No, nothing," he replied.

Signor Reginaudo patted me on the shoulder, the Signora opened the blinds to let the sun in. Then they took me around the house.

He was wearing pink-striped pajama trousers tied over his fat little stomach, and a straw hat on his bald head. She wore a faded dressing gown, which opened every now and then to reveal the shoulder straps of her undershirt; the hair around her big red face was fair, dry, curly, and disheveled. They both talked loudly and expansively; every corner of their house had a story which they recounted, repeating and interrupting each other with gestures and exclamations as if each episode had been a huge joke. In one place they had put down Arfanax diluted two to a thousand and the ants had vanished for two days but returned on the third day; then he had used a concentrate of ten to a thousand, but the ants had simply avoided that part and circled around by the doorframe; they had isolated another corner with Crisotan powder, but the wind blew it away and they used three kilos a day; on the stairs they had tried Petrocid, which seemed at first to kill them at one blow, but instead it had only sent them to sleep; in another corner they put down Formikill and the ants went on passing over it, then one morning they found a mouse poisoned there; in one spot they had put down liquid Zimofosf, which had acted as a definite blockade, but his wife had put Italmac powder on top which had acted as an antidote and completely nullified the effect.

Our neighbors used their house and garden as a battle-field, and their passion was to trace lines beyond which the ants could not pass, to discover the new detours they made, and to try out new mixtures and powders, each of which was linked to the memory of some strange episode or comic occurrence, so that one of them only had to pronounce a name "Arsepit! Mirxidol!" for them both to burst out laughing with winks and comments. As for the actual killing of the ants, that, if they had ever attempted it, they seemed to have given up, seeing that their efforts were useless; all they tried to do was bar them from certain passages and turn them aside, frighten them or keep them at bay. They always had a new labyrinth traced out with different substances which they prepared from day to day, and for this game ants were a necessary element.

"There's nothing else to be done with the creatures, nothing," they said, "unless one deals with them like the captain . . ."

"Ah, yes, we certainly spend a lot of money on these insecticides," they said. "The captain's system is much more economical, you know."

"Of course, we can't say we've defeated the Argentine ant yet," they added, "but d'you really think that captain is on the right road? I doubt it."

"Excuse me," I asked. "But who is the captain?"

"Captain Brauni; don't you know him? Oh, of course, you only arrived yesterday! He's our neighbor there on the right, in that little white villa . . . an inventor. . . ." They laughed. "He's invented a system to exterminate the Argentine ant . . . lots of systems, in fact. And he's still perfecting them. Go and see him."

The Reginaudos stood there, plump and sly among their few square yards of garden which was daubed all over with streaks and splashes of dark liquids, sprinkled with greenish powder, encumbered with watering cans, fumigators, masonry basins filled with some indigo-colored preparation; in the disordered flower beds were a few little rosebushes covered with insecticide from the tips of the leaves to the roots. The Reginaudos raised contented and amused eyes to the limpid sky. Talking to them, I found myself slightly heartened; although the ants were not just something to laugh at, as they seemed to think, neither were they so terribly serious, anything to lose heart about. "Oh, the ants!" I now thought. "Just ants after all! What harm can a few ants do?" Now I'd go back to my wife and tease her a bit: "What on earth d'you think you've seen, with those ants . . . ?"

I was mentally preparing a talk in this tone while returning across our piece of ground with my arms full of cartons and tins lent by our neighbors for us to choose the ones that wouldn't harm the baby, who put everything in his mouth. But when I saw my wife outside the house holding the baby, her eyes glassy and her cheeks hollow, and realized the battle she must have fought, I lost all desire to smile and joke.

"At last you've come back," she said, and her quiet tone impressed me more painfully than the angry accent I had expected. "I didn't know what to do here any more . . . if you saw . . . I really didn't know . . ."

"Look, now we can try this," I said to her, "and this and this and this . . ." and I put down my cans on the step in front of the house, and at once began hurriedly explaining how they were to be used, almost afraid of seeing too much hope rising in her eyes, not wanting either to deceive or undeceive her. Now I had another idea: I wanted to go at once and see that Captain Brauni.

"Do it the way I've explained; I'll be back in a minute."

"You're going away again? Where are you off to?"

"To another neighbor's. He has a system. You'll see soon."

And I ran off toward a metal fence covered with ramblers bounding our land to the right. The sun was behind a cloud. I looked through the fence and saw a little white villa surrounded by a tiny neat garden, with gravel paths encircling flower beds, bordered by wrought iron painted green as in public gardens, and in the middle of every flower bed a little black orange or lemon tree.

Everything was quiet, shady, and still. I was standing there, uncertain whether to go away, when, bending over a well-clipped hedge, I saw a head covered with a shapeless white linen beach hat, pulled forward to a wavy brim above a pair of steel-framed glasses on a spongy nose, and then a sharp flashing smile of false teeth, also made of steel. He was a thin, shriveled man in a pullover, with trousers clamped at the ankles by bicycle clips, and sandals on his feet. He went up to examine the trunk of one of the orange trees, looking silent and circumspect, still with his tight-lipped smile. I looked out from behind the rambler and called: "Good day, Captain." The man raised his head with a start, no longer smiling, and gave me a cold stare.

"Excuse me, are you Captain Brauni?" I asked him. The man nodded. "I'm the new neighbor, you know, who's rented the Casa Laureri. . . . May I trouble you for a moment, since I've heard that your system . . ."

The captain raised a finger and beckoned me to come nearer; I jumped through a gap in the iron fence. The captain was still holding up his finger, while pointing with the other hand to the spot he was observing. I saw that hanging from the tree, perpendicular to the trunk, was a short iron wire. At the end of the wire hung a piece—it seemed to me —of fish remains, and in the middle was a bulge at an acute angle pointing downward. A stream of ants was going to and fro on the trunk and the wire. Underneath the end of the wire was hanging a sort of meat can.

"The ants," explained the captain, "attracted by the smell of fish, run across the piece of wire; as you see, they can go to and fro on it without bumping into each other. But it's that *V* turn that is dangerous; when an ant going up meets one coming down on the turn of the *V*, they both stop, and the smell of the gasoline in this can stuns them; they try to go on their way but bump into each other, fall, and are drowned in the gasoline. Tic, tic." (This "tic, tic" accompanied the fall of two ants.) "Tic, tic, tic . . ." continued the captain with his steely, stiff smile; and every "tic" accompanied the fall of an ant into the can where, on the surface of an inch of gasoline, lay a black crust of shapeless insect bodies.

"An average of forty ants are killed per minute," said Captain Brauni, "twenty-four hundred per hour. Naturally, the gasoline must be kept clean, otherwise the dead ants cover it and the ones that fall in afterward can save themselves."

I could not take my eyes off that thin but regular trickle of ants dropping off; many of them got over the dangerous point and returned dragging bits of fish back with them by the teeth, but there was always one which stopped at that point, waved its antennae, and then plunged into the depths. Captain Brauni, with a fixed stare behind his lenses, did not miss the slightest movement of the insects; at every fall he gave a tiny uncontrollable start and the tightly stretched corners of his almost lipless mouth twitched. Often he could not resist putting out his hands, either to correct the angle of the wire or to stir the gasoline around the crust of dead ants on the sides, or even to give his instruments a little shake to accelerate the victims' fall. But this last gesture must have seemed to him almost like breaking the rules, for he quickly drew back his hand and looked at me as if to justify his action.

"This is an improved model," he said, leading me to another tree from which hung a wire with a horsehair tied to the top of the V: the ants thought they could save themselves on the horsehair, but the smell of the gasoline and the unexpectedly tenuous support confused them to the point of making the fatal drop. This expedient of the horsehair or bristle was applied to many other traps that the captain showed me: a third piece of wire would suddenly end in a piece of thin horsehair, and the ants would be confused by the change and lose their balance; he had even constructed a trap by which the corner was reached over a bridge made of a half-broken bristle, which opened under the weight of the ant and let it fall in the gasoline.

Applied with mathematical precision to every tree, every piece of tubing, every balustrade and column in this silent and neat garden, were wire contraptions with cans of gasoline underneath, and the standard-trained rosebushes and latticework of ramblers seemed only a careful camouflage for this parade of executions.

"Aglaura!" cried the captain, going up to the kitchen door, and to me: "Now I'll show you our catch for the last few days."

Out of the door came a tall, thin, pale women with frightened, malevolent eyes, and a handkerchief knotted down over her forehead.

"Show our neighbor the sack," said Brauni, and I realized she was not a servant but the captain's wife, and greeted her with a nod and a murmur, but she did not reply. She went into the house and came out again dragging a heavy sack along the ground, her muscular arms showing a greater strength than I had attributed to her at first glance. Through the half-closed door I could see a pile of sacks like this one stacked about; the woman had disappeared, still without saying a word.

The captain opened the mouth of the sack; it looked as if it contained garden loam or chemical manure, but he put his arm in and brought out a handful of what seemed to be coffee grounds and let this trickle into his other hand; they were dead ants, a soft red-black sand of dead ants all rolled up in tight little balls, reduced to spots in which one could no longer distinguish the head from the legs. They gave out a pungent acid smell. In the house there were hundred-weights, pyramids of sacks like this one, all full.

"It's incredible," I said. "You've exterminated all of these, so . . ."

"No," said the captain calmly. "It's no use killing the worker ants. There are ants' nests everywhere with queen ants that breed millions of others."

"What then?"

I squatted down beside the sack; he was seated on a step below me and to speak to me had to raise his head; the shapeless brim of his white hat covered the whole of his forehead and part of his round spectacles.

"The queens must be starved. If you reduce to a minimum the number of workers taking food to the ants' nests, the queens will be left without enough to eat. And I tell you that one day we'll see the queens come out of their ants' nests in high summer and crawl around searching for food with their own claws. . . . That'll be the end of them all, and then . . ."

He shut the mouth of the sack with an excited gesture and got up. I got up too. "But some people think they can solve it by letting the ants escape." He threw a glance toward the Reginaudos' little house, and showed his steel teeth in a contemptuous laugh. "And there are even those who prefer fattening them up. . . . That's one way of dealing with them, isn't it?"

I did not understand his second allusion.

"Who?" I asked. "Why should anyone want to fatten them up?"

"Hasn't the ant man been to you?"

What man did he mean? "I don't know," I said. "I don't think so. . . ."

"Don't worry, he'll come to you too. He usually comes on Thursdays, so if he wasn't here this morning he will be in the afternoon. To give the ants a tonic, ha, ha!"

I smiled to please him, but did not follow. Then as I had come to him with a purpose I said: "I'm sure yours is the best possible system. D'you think I could try it at my place too?"

"Just tell me which model you prefer," said Brauni, and led me back into the garden. There were numbers of his inventions that I had not yet seen. Swinging wire which when loaded with ants made contact with a battery that electrocuted the lot; anvils and hammers covered with honey which clashed together at the release of a spring and squashed all the ants left in between; wheels with teeth which the ants themselves put in motion, tearing their brethren to pieces until they in their turn were churned up by the pressure of those coming after. I couldn't get used to the idea of so much art and perseverance being needed to carry out such a simple operation as catching ants; but I realized that the important thing was to carry on continually and methodically. Then I felt discouraged as no one, it seemed to me, could ever equal this neighbor of ours in terrible determination.

"Perhaps one of the simpler models would be best for us," I said, and Brauni snorted, I didn't know whether from approval or sympathy with the modesty of my ambition.

"I must think a bit about it," he said. "I'll make some sketches."

There was nothing else left for me to do but thank him and take my leave. I jumped back over the hedge; my house, infested as it was, I felt for the first time to be really my home, a place where one returned saying: "Here I am at last."

But at home the baby had eaten the insecticide and my wife was in despair.

"Don't worry, it's not poisonous!" I quickly said.

No, it wasn't poisonous, but it wasn't good to eat either; our son was screaming with pain. He had to be made to vomit; he vomited in the kitchen, which at once filled with ants again, and my wife had just cleaned it up. We washed the floor, calmed the baby, and put him to sleep in the basket, isolated him all around with insect powder, and covered him with a mosquito net tied tight, so that if he awoke he couldn't get up and eat any more of the stuff.

My wife had done the shopping but had not been able to save the basket from the ants, so everything had to be washed first, even the sardines in oil and the cheese, and each ant sticking to them picked off one by one. I helped her, chopped the wood, tidied the kitchen, and fixed the stove while she cleaned the vegetables. But it was impossible to stand still in one place; every minute either she or I jumped and said: "Ouch! They're biting," and we had to scratch ourselves and rub off the ants or put our arms and legs under the faucet. We did not know where to set the table; inside it would attract more ants, outside we'd be covered with ants in no time. We ate standing up, moving about, and everything tasted of ants, partly from the ones still left in the food and partly because our hands were impregnated with their smell.

After eating I made a tour of the piece of land, smoking a cigarette. From the Reginaudos' came a tinkling of knives and forks; I went over and saw them sitting at table under an umbrella, looking shiny and calm, with checked napkins tied around their necks, eating a custard and drinking glasses of clear wine. I wished them a good appetite and they invited me to join them. But around the table I saw sacks and cans of insecticide, and everything covered with nets sprinkled with yellowish or whitish powder, and that smell of chemicals rose to my nostrils. I thanked them and said I no longer had any appetite, which was true. The Reginaudos' radio was playing softly and they were chattering in high voices, pretending to celebrate.

From the steps which I'd gone up to greet them I could also see a piece of the Braunis' garden; the captain must already have finished eating; he was coming out of his house with his cup of coffee, sipping and glancing around, obviously to see if all his instruments of torture were in action and if the ants' death agonies were continuing with their usual regularity. Suspended between two trees I saw a white hammock and realized that the bony, disagreeable-looking Signora Aglaura must be lying in it, though I could see only a wrist and a hand waving a ribbed fan. The hammock ropes were suspended in a system of strange rings, which must certainly have been some sort of defense against the ants; or perhaps the hammock itself was a trap for the ants, with the captain's wife put there as bait.

I did not want to discuss my visit to the Braunis with the Reginaudos, as I knew they would only have made the ironic comments that seemed usual in the relations between our neighbors. I looked up at Signora Mauro's garden above us on the crest of the hills, and at her villa surmounted by a revolving weathercock. "I wonder if Signora Mauro has ants up there too," I said.

The Reginaudos' gaiety seemed rather more subdued during their meal; they only gave a little quiet laugh or two and said no more than: "Ha, ha, she must have them too. Ha, ha, yes, she must have them, lots of them. . . ."

My wife called me back to the house, as she wanted to put a mattress on the table and try to get a little sleep. With the mattresses on the floor it was impossible to prevent the ants from crawling up, but with the table we just had to isolate the four legs to keep them off, for a bit at least. She lay down to rest and I went out, with the thought of looking for some people who might know of some job for me, but in fact because I longed to move about and get out of the rut of my thoughts.

But as I went along the road, things all around seemed different from yesterday; in every kitchen garden, in every house I sensed streams of ants climbing the walls, covering the fruit trees, wriggling their antennae toward everything sweet or greasy; and my newly trained eyes now noticed at once mattresses put outside houses to beat because the ants had got into them, a spray of insecticide in an old woman's hand, a saucerful of poison, and then, straining my eyes, the rows of ants marching imperturbably around the door frames.

Yet this had been Uncle Augusto's ideal countryside. Unloading sacks, an hour for one employer and an hour for another, eating on the benches at the inn, going around in the evening in search of gaiety and a mouth organ, sleeping wherever he happened to be, wherever it was cool and soft, what bother could the ants have been to him?

As I walked along I tried to imagine myself as Uncle Augusto and to move along the road as he would have done on an afternoon like this. Of course, being like Uncle Augusto meant first being like him physically: squat and sturdy, that is, with rather monkeylike arms that opened and remained suspended in mid-air in an extravagant gesture, and short legs that stumbled when he turned to look at a girl, and a voice which when he got excited repeated the local slang all out of tune with his own accent. In him body and soul were all one; how nice it would have been, gloomy and worried as I was, to have been able to move and joke like Uncle Augusto. I could always pretend to be him mentally, though, and say to myself: "What a sleep I'll have in that hayloft! What a bellyful of sausage and wine I'll have at the inn!" I imagined myself pretending to stroke the cats I saw, then shouting "Booo!" to frighten them unexpectedly; and calling out to the servant girls: "Hey, would you like me to come and give you a hand, Signorina?" But the game wasn't much fun; the more I tried to imagine how simple life was for Uncle Augusto here, the more I realized he was a different type, a man who never had my worries: a home to set up, a permanent job to find, an ailing baby, a long-faced wife, and a bed and kitchen full of ants.

I entered the inn where we had already been, and asked the girl in the white sweater if the men I'd talked to the day before had come yet. It was shady and cool in there; perhaps it wasn't a place for ants. I sat down to wait for those men, as she suggested, and asked, looking as casual as I could: "So you haven't any ants here, then?"

She was passing a duster over the counter. "Oh, people come and go here, no one's ever paid any attention."

"But what about you who live here all the time?"

The girl shrugged her shoulders. "I'm grown up, why should I be frightened of ants?"

Her air of dismissing the ants, as if they were something to be ashamed of, irritated me more and more, and I insisted: "But don't you put any poison down?"

"The best poison against ants," said a man sitting at another table, who, I noted now, was one of those friends of Uncle Augusto's to whom I'd spoken the evening before, "is this," and he raised his glass and drank it in one gulp.

Others came in and wanted to stand me a drink as they hadn't been able to put me on to any jobs. We talked about Uncle Augusto and one of them asked: "And what's that old *lingera* up to?" *"Lingera"* is a local word meaning vagabond and scamp, and they all seemed to approve of this definition of him and to hold my uncle in great esteem as a *lingera*. I was a little confused at this reputation being attributed to a man whom I knew to be in fact considerate and modest, in spite of his disorganized way of life. But perhaps this was part of the boasting, exaggerated attitude common to all these people, and it occurred to me in a confused sort of way that this was somehow linked with the ants, that pretending they lived in a world of great movement and adventure was a way of insulating themselves from petty annoyances.

What prevented me from entering their state of mind, I was thinking on my way home, was my wife, who had always been opposed to any fantasy. And I thought what an influence she had had on my life, and how nowadays I could never get drunk on words and ideas any more.

She met me on the doorstep looking rather alarmed, and said: "Listen, there's a surveyor here." I, who still had in my ears the sound of superiority of those blusterers at the inn, said almost without listening: "What now, a surveyor . . . Well, I'll just . . ."

She went on: "A surveyor's come to take measurements." I did not understand and went in. "Ah, now I see. It's the captain!"

It was Captain Brauni who was taking measurements with a yellow tape measure, to set up one of his traps in our house. I introduced him to my wife and thanked him for his kindness.

"I wanted to have a look at the possibilities here," he said. "Everything must be done in a strictly mathematical way." He even measured the basket where the baby was sleeping, and woke it up. The child was frightened at seeing the yellow yardstick leveled over his head and began to cry. My wife tried to put him to sleep again. The baby's crying made the captain nervous, though I tried to distract him. Luckily, he heard his wife calling him and went out. Signora Aglaura was leaning over the hedge and shouting: "Come here! Come here! There's a visitor! Yes, the ant man!"

Brauni gave me a glance and a meaningful smile from his thin lips, and excused himself for having to return to his house so soon. "Now, he'll come to you too," he said, pointing toward the place where this mysterious ant man was to be found. "You'll soon see," and he went away.

I did not want to find myself face to face with this ant man without knowing exactly who he was and what he had come to do. I went to the steps that led to Reginaudo's land; our neighbor was just at that moment returning home; he was wearing a white coat and a straw hat, and was loaded with sacks and cartons. I said to him: "Tell me, has the ant man been to you yet?"

"I don't know," said Reginaudo, "I've just got back, but I think he must have, because I see molasses everywhere. Claudia!"

His wife leaned out and said: "Yes, yes, he'll come to the Casa Laureri too, but don't expect him to do very much!"

As if I was expecting anything at all! I asked: "But who sent this man?"

"Who sent him?" repeated Reginaudo. "He's the man from the Argentine Ant Control Corporation, their representative who comes and puts molasses all over the gardens and houses. Those little plates over there, do you see them?"

My wife said: "Poisoned molasses . . ." and gave a little laugh as if she expected trouble.

"Does it kill them?" These questions of mine were just a deprecating joke. I knew it all already. Every now and then everything would seem on the point of clearing up, then complications would begin all over again.

Signor Reginaudo shook his head as if I'd said something improper. "Oh no . . . just minute doses of poison, you understand . . . ants love sugary molasses. The worker ants take it back to the nest and feed the queens with these little doses of poison, so that sooner or later they're supposed to die from poisoning."

I did not want to ask if, sooner or later, they really did die. I realized that Signor Reginaudo was informing me of this proceeding in the tone of one who personally holds a different view but feels that he should give an objective and respectful account of official opinion. His wife, however, with the habitual intolerance of women, was quite open about showing her aversion to the molasses system and interrupted her husband's remarks with little malicious laughs and ironic comments; this attitude of hers must have seemed to him out of place or too open, for he tried by his voice and manner to attenuate her defeatism, though not actually contradicting her entirely—perhaps because in private he said the same things, or worse—by making little compensating remarks such as: "Come now, you exaggerate, Claudia. . . . It's certainly not very effective, but it may help. . . . Then, they do it for nothing. One must wait a year or two before judging. . . ."

"A year or two? They've been putting that stuff down for twenty years, and every year the ants multiply."

Signor Reginaudo, rather than contradict her, preferred to turn the conversation to other services performed by the Corporation; and he told me about the boxes of manure which the ant man put in the gardens for the queens to go and lay their eggs in, and how they then came and took them away to burn.

I realized that Signor Reginaudo's tone was the best to use in explaining matters to my wife, who is suspicious and pessimistic by nature, and when I got back home I reported what our neighbor had said, taking care not to praise the system as in any way miraculous or speedy, but also avoiding Signora Claudia's ironic comments. My wife is one of those women who, when she goes by train, for example, thinks that the timetable, the make-up of the train, the requests of the ticket collectors, are all stupid and ill planned, without any possible justification, but to be accepted with submissive rancor; so though she considered this business of molasses to be absurd and ridiculous, she made ready for the visit of the ant man (who, I gathered, was called Signor Baudino), intending to make no protest or useless request for help.

The man entered our plot of land without asking permission, and we found ourselves face to face while we were still talking about him, which caused rather an unpleasant embarrassment. He was a little man of about fifty, in a worn, faded black suit, with rather a drunkard's face, and hair that was still dark, parted like a child's. Half-closed lids, a rather greasy little smile, reddish skin around his eyes and at the sides of his nose, prepared us for the intonations of a clucking, rather priestlike voice with a strong lilt of dialect. A nervous tic made the wrinkles pulsate at the corner of his mouth and nose.

If I describe Signor Baudino in such detail, it's to try to define the strange impression that he made on us; but was it strange, really? For it seemed to us that we'd have picked him out among thousands as the ant man. He had large, hairy hands; in one he held a sort of coffeepot and in the other a pile of little earthenware plates. He told us about the molasses he had to put down, and his voice betrayed a lazy indifference to the job; even the soft and dragging way he had of pronouncing the word "molasses" showed both disdain for the straits we were in and the complete lack of faith with which he carried out his task. I noticed that my wife was displaying exemplary calm as she showed him the main places where the ants passed. For myself, seeing him move so hesitantly, repeating again and again those few gestures of filling the dishes one after the other, nearly made me lose my patience. Watching him like that, I realized why he had made such a strange impression on me at first sight: he looked like an ant. It's difficult to tell exactly why, but he certainly did; perhaps it was because of the dull black of his clothes and hair, perhaps because of the proportions of that squat body of his, or the trembling at the corners of his mouth corresponding to the continuous quiver of antennae and claws. There was, however, one characteristic of the ant which he did not have, and that was their continuous busy movement. Signor Baudino moved slowly and awkwardly, as he now began daubing the house in an aimless way with a brush dipped in molasses.

As I followed the man's movements with increasing irritation I noticed that my wife was no longer with me; I looked around and saw her in a corner of the garden where the hedge of the Reginaudos' little house joined that of the Braunis'. Leaning over their respective hedges were Signora Claudia and Signora Aglaura, deep in talk, with my wife standing in the middle listening. Signor Baudino was now working on the yard at the back of the house, where he could mess around as much as he liked without having to be watched, so I went up to the women and heard Signora Brauni holding forth to the accompaniment of sharp angular gestures.

"He's come to give the ants a tonic, that man has; a tonic, not poison at all!"

Signora Reginaudo now chimed in, rather mellifluously: "What will the employees of the Corporation do when there are no more ants? So what can you expect of them, my dear Signora?"

"They just fatten the ants, that's what they do!" concluded Signora Aglaura angrily.

My wife stood listening quietly, as both the neighbors' remarks were addressed to her, but the way in which she was dilating her nostrils and curling her lips told me how furious she was at the deceit she was being forced to put up with. And I, too, I must say, found myself very near believing that this was more than women's gossip.

"And what about the boxes of manure for the eggs?"

went on Signora Reginaudo. "They take them away, but do you think they'll burn them? Of course not!"

"Claudia, Claudia!" I heard her husband calling. Obviously these indiscreet remarks of his wife made him feel uneasy. Signora Reginaudo left us with an "Excuse me," in which vibrated a note of disdain for her husband's conventionality, while I thought I heard a kind of sardonic laugh echoing back from over the other hedge, where I caught sight of Captain Brauni walking up the graveled paths and correcting the slant of his traps. One of the earthenware dishes just filled by Signor Baudino lay overturned and smashed at his feet by a kick which might have been accidental or intended.

I don't know what my wife had brewing inside her against the ant man as we were returning toward the house; probably at that moment I should have done nothing to stop her, and might even have supported her. But on glancing around the outside and inside of the house, we realized that Signor Baudino had disappeared; and I remembered hearing our gate creaking and shutting as we came along. He must have gone that moment without saying good-by, leaving behind him those bowls of sticky, reddish molasses, which spread an unpleasant sweet smell, completely different from that of the ants, but somehow linked to it, I could not say how.

Since our son was sleeping, we thought that now was the moment to go up and see Signora Mauro. We had to go and visit her, not only as a duty call but to ask her for the key of a certain storeroom. The real reasons, though, why we were making this call so soon were to remonstrate with her for having rented us a place invaded with ants without warning us in any way, and chiefly to find out how our landlady defended herself against this scourge.

Signora Mauro's villa had a big garden running up the slope under tall palms with yellowed fanlike leaves. A winding path led to the house, which was all glass verandas and dormer windows, with a rusty weathercock turning creakily on its hinge on top of the roof, far less responsive to the wind than the palm leaves which waved and rustled at every gust.

My wife and I climbed the path and gazed down from the balustrade at the little house where we lived and which was still unfamiliar to us, at our patch of uncultivated land and the Reginaudos' garden looking like a warehouse yard, at the Braunis' garden looking as regular as a cemetery. And standing up there we could forget that all those places were black with ants; now we could see how they might have been without that menace which none of us could get away from even for an instant. At this distance it looked almost like a paradise, but the more we gazed down the more we pitied our life there, as if living in that wretched narrow valley we could never get away from our wretched narrow problems.

Signora Mauro was very old, thin, and tall. She received us in half darkness, sitting on a high-backed chair by a little table which opened to hold sewing things and writing materials. She was dressed in black, except for a white mannish collar; her thin face was lightly powdered, and her hair drawn severely back. She immediately handed us the key she had promised us the day before, but did not ask if we were all right, and this—it seemed to us—was a sign that she was already expecting our complaints.

"But the ants that there are down there, Signora . . ." said my wife in a tone which this time I wished had been less humble and resigned. Although she can be quite hard and often even aggressive, my wife is seized by shyness every now and then, and seeing her at these moments always makes me feel uncomfortable too.

I came to her support, and assuming a tone full of resentment, said: "You've rented us a house, Signora, which if I'd known about all those ants, I must tell you frankly . . ." and stopped there, thinking that I'd been clear enough.

The Signora did not even raise her eyes. "The house has been unoccupied for a long time," she said. "It's understandable that there are a few Argentine ants in it . . . they get wherever . . . wherever things aren't properly cleaned. You," she turned to me, "kept me waiting for four months before giving me a reply. If you'd taken the place immediately, there wouldn't be any ants by now."

We looked at the room, almost in darkness because of the half-closed blinds and curtains, at the high walls covered with antique tapestry, at the dark, inlaid furniture with the silver vases and teapots gleaming on top, and it seemed to us that this darkness and these heavy hangings served to hide the presence of streams of ants which must certainly be running through the old house from foundations to roof.

"And here . . ." said my wife, in an insinuating, almost ironic tone, "you haven't any ants?"

Signora Mauro drew in her lips. "No," she said curtly; and then as if she felt she was not being believed, explained: "Here we keep everything clean and shining as a mirror. As soon as any ants enter the garden, we realize it and deal with them at once."

"How?" my wife and I quickly asked in one voice, feeling only hope and curiosity now.

"Oh," said the Signora, shrugging her shoulders, "we chase them away, chase them away with brooms." At that moment her expression of studied impassiveness was shaken as if by a spasm of physical pain, and we saw that, as she sat,

173

she suddenly moved her weight to another side of the chair and arched in her waist. Had it not contradicted her affirmations I'd have said that an Argentine ant was passing under her clothes and had just given her a bite; one or perhaps several ants were surely crawling up her body and making her itch, for in spite of her efforts not to move from the chair it was obvious that she was unable to remain calm and composed as before—she sat there tensely, while her face showed signs of sharper and sharper suffering.

"But that bit of land in front of us is black with 'em," I said hurriedly, "and however clean we keep the house, they come from the garden in their thousands. . . ."

"Of course," said the Signora, her thin hand closing over the arm of the chair, "of course it's rough uncultivated ground that makes the ants increase so; I intended to put the land in order four months ago. You made me wait, and now the damage is done; it's not only damaged you, but everyone else around, because the ants breed . . ."

"Don't they breed up here too?" asked my wife, almost smiling.

"No, not here!" said Signora Mauro, going pale, then, still holding her right arm against the side of the chair, she began making a little rotating movement of the shoulder and rubbing her elbow against her ribs.

It occurred to me that the darkness, the ornaments, the size of the room, and her proud spirit were this woman's defenses against the ants, the reason why she was stronger than we were in face of them; but that everything we saw around us, beginning with her sitting there, was covered with ants even more pitiless than ours; some kind of African termite, perhaps, which destroyed everything and left only the husks, so that all that remained of this house were tapestries and curtains almost in powder, all on the point of crumbling into bits before her eyes.

"We really came to ask you if you could give us some advice on how to get rid of the pests," said my wife, who was now completely self-possessed.

"Keep the house clean and dig away at the ground. There's no other remedy. Work, just work," and she got to her feet, the sudden decision to say good-by to us coinciding with an instinctive start, as if she could keep still no longer. Then she composed herself and a shadow of relief passed over her pale face.

We went down through the garden, and my wife said: "Anyway, let's hope the baby hasn't waked up." I, too, was thinking of the baby. Even before we reached the house we heard him crying. We ran, took him in our arms, and tried to quiet him, but he went on crying shrilly. An ant had got into his ear; we could not understand at first why he cried so desperately without any apparent reason. My wife had said at once: "It must be an ant!" but I could not understand why he went on crying so, as we could find no ants on him or any signs of bites or irritation, and we'd undressed and carefully inspected him. We found some in the basket, however; I'd done my very best to isolate it properly, but we had overlooked the ant man's molasses—one of the clumsy streaks made by Signor Baudino seemed to have been put down on purpose to attract the insects up from the floor to the child's cot.

What with the baby's tears and my wife's cries, we had attracted all the neighboring women to the house: Signora Reginaudo, who was really very kind and sweet, Signora Brauni, who, I must say, did everything she could to help us, and other women I'd never seen before. They all gave ceaseless advice: to pour warm oil in his ear, make him hold his mouth open, blow his nose, and I don't know what else. They screamed and shouted and ended by giving us more trouble than help, although they'd been a certain comfort at first; and the more they fussed around our baby the more bitter we all felt against the ant man. My wife had blamed and cursed him to the four winds of heaven; and the neighbors all agreed with her that the man deserved all that was coming to him, and that he was doing all he could to help the ants increase so as not to lose his job, and that he was perfectly capable of having done this on purpose, because now he was always on the side of the ants and not on that of human beings. Exaggeration, of course, but in all this excitement, with the baby crying, I agreed too, and if I'd laid hands on Signor Baudino then I couldn't say what I'd have done to him either.

The warm oil got the ant out; the baby, half stunned with crying, took up a celluloid toy, waved it about, sucked it, and decided to forget us. I, too, felt the same need to be on my own and relax my nerves, but the women were still continuing their diatribe against Baudino, and they told my wife that he could probably be found in an enclosure nearby, where he had his warehouse. My wife exclaimed: "Ah, I'll go and see him, yes, go and see him and give him what he deserves!"

Then they formed a small procession, with my wife at the head and I, naturally, beside her, without giving any opinion on the usefulness of the undertaking, and other women who had incited my wife following and sometimes overtaking her to show her the way. Signora Claudia offered to hold the baby and waved to us from the gate; I realized later that Signora Aglaura was not with us either, although she had declared herself to be one of Baudino's most violent enemies, and that we were accompanied by a little group of women we had not seen before. We went along a sort of alley, flanked by wooden hovels, chicken coops, and vegetable gardens half full of rubbish. One or two of the women, in spite of all they'd said, stopped when they got to their own homes, stood on the threshold excitedly pointing out our direction, then retired inside calling to the dirty children playing on the ground, or disappeared to feed the chickens. Only a couple of women followed us as far as Baudino's enclosure; but when the door opened after heavy knocks by my wife we found that she and I were the only ones to go in, though we felt ourselves followed by the other women's eyes from windows or chicken coops; they seemed to be continuing to incite us, but in very low voices and without showing themselves at all.

The ant man was in the middle of his warehouse, a shack three-quarters destroyed, to whose one surviving wooden wall was tacked a yellow notice with letters a foot and a half long: "Argentine Ant Control Corporation." Lying all around were piles of those dishes for molasses and tins and bottles of every description, all in a sort of rubbish heap full of bits of paper with fish remains and other refuse, so that it immediately occurred to one that this was the source of all the ants of the area. Signor Baudino stood in front of us half smiling in an irritating questioning way, showing the gaps in his teeth.

"You," my wife attacked him, recovering herself after a moment of hesitation. "You should be ashamed of yourself! Why d'you come to our house and dirty everything and let the baby get an ant in his ear with your molasses?"

She had her fists under his face, and Signor Baudino, without ceasing to give that decayed-looking smile of his, made the movements of a wild animal trying to keep its escape open, at the same time shrugging his shoulders and glancing and winking around to me, since there was no one else in sight, as if to say: "She's bats." But his voice only uttered generalities and soft denials like: "No . . . No . . . Of course not."

"Why does everyone say that you give the ants a tonic instead of poisoning them?" shouted my wife, so he slipped out of the door into the road with my wife following him and screaming abuse. Now the shrugging and winking of Signor Baudino were addressed to the women of the surrounding hovels, and it seemed to me that they were playing some kind of double game, agreeing to be witnesses for him that my wife was insulting him; and yet when my wife looked at them they incited her, with sharp little jerks of the head and movements of the brooms, to attack the ant man. I did not intervene; what could I have done? I certainly did not want to lay hands on the little man, as my wife's fury with him was already roused enough; nor could I try to moderate it, as I did not want to defend Baudino. At last my wife in another burst of anger cried: "You've done my baby harm!" grasped him by his collar, and shook him hard.

I was just about to throw myself on them and separate them; but without touching her, he twisted around with movements that were becoming more and more antlike, until he managed to break away. Then he went off with a clumsy, running step, stopped, pulled himself together, and went on again, still shrugging his shoulders and muttering phrases like: "But what behavior . . . But who . . ." and making a gesture as if to say "She's crazy," to the people in the nearby hovels. From those people, the moment my wife threw herself on him, there rose an indistinct but confused mutter which stopped as soon as the man freed himself, then started up again in phrases not so much of protest and threat as of complaint and almost of supplication or sympathy, shouted out as if they were proud proclamations. "The ants are eating us alive. . . . Ants in the bed, ants in the dishes, ants every day, ants every night. We've little enough to eat anyway and have to feed them too. . . ."

I had taken my wife by the arm. She was still shaking her fist every now and again and shouting: "That's not the last of it! We know who is swindling whom! We know whom to thank!" and other threatening phrases which did not echo back, as the windows and doors of the hovels on our path closed again, and the inhabitants returned to their wretched lives with the ants.

So it was a sad return, as could have been foreseen. But what had particularly disappointed me was the way those women had behaved. I swore I'd never go around complaining about ants again in my life. I longed to shut myself up in silent tortured pride like Signora Mauro—but she was rich and we were poor. I had not yet found any solution to how we could go on living in these parts; and it seemed to me that none of the people here, who seemed so superior a short time ago, had found it, or were even on the way to finding it either.

We reached home; the baby was sucking his toy. My wife sat down on a chair. I looked at the ant-infested field and hedges, and beyond them at the cloud of insect powder rising from Signor Reginaudo's garden; and to the right there was the shady silence of the captain's garden, with that continuous dripping of his victims. This was my new home. I took my wife and child and said: "Let's go for a walk, let's go down to the sea."

It was evening. We went along alleys and streets of steps. The sun beat down on a sharp corner of the old town, on gray, porous stone, with lime-washed cornices to the windows and roofs green with moss. The town opened like a fan, undulating over slopes and hills, and the space between was full of limpid air, copper-colored at this hour. Our child was turning around in amazement at everything, and we had to pretend to take part in his marveling; it was a way of bringing us together, of reminding us of the mild flavor that life has at moments, and of reconciling us to the passing days.

We met old women balancing great baskets resting on head pads, walking rigidly with straight backs and lowered eyes; and in a nuns' garden a group of sewing girls ran along a railing to see a toad in a basin and said: "How awful!"; and behind an iron gate, under the wistaria, some young girls dressed in white were throwing a beach ball to and fro with a blind man; and a half-naked youth with a beard and hair down to his shoulders was gathering prickly pears from an old cactus with a forked stick; and sad and spectacled children were making soap bubbles at the window of a rich house; it was the hour when the bell sounded in the old folks' home and they began climbing up the steps, one behind the other with their sticks, their straw hats on their heads, each talking to himself; and then there were two telephone workers, and one was holding a ladder and saying to the other on the pole: "Come on down, time's up, we'll finish the job tomorrow."

And so we reached the port and the sea. There was also a line of palm trees and some stone benches. My wife and I sat down and the baby was quiet. My wife said: "There are no ants here." I replied: "And there's a fresh wind; it's pleasant."

The sea rose and fell against the rocks of the mole, making the fishing boats sway, and dark-skinned men were filling them with red nets and lobster pots for the evening's fishing. The water was calm, with just a slight continual change of color, blue and black, darker farthest away. I thought of the expanses of water like this, of the infinite grains of soft sand down there at the bottom of the sea where the currents leave white shells washed clean by the waves.